BEOWULF

Supplementary material written by Frederic Will
Series edited by Cynthia Brantley Johnson

SIMON & SCHUSTER PAPERBACKS
NEW YORK LONDON TORONTO SYDNEY

Simon & Schuster Paperbacks
A Division of Simon & Schuster, Inc.
1230 Avenue of the Americas
New York, NY 10020

This book is a work of fiction. Names, characters, places, and
incidents either are products of the author's imagination or are
used fictitiously. Any resemblance to actual events or locales or
persons, living or dead, is entirely coincidental.

Supplementary materials copyright © 2005 by Simon & Schuster, Inc.

This Simon & Schuster paperback edition November 2009

SIMON & SCHUSTER PAPERBACKS and colophon are
registered trademarks of Simon & Schuster, Inc.

For information regarding special discounts for bulk purchases,
please contact Simon & Schuster Special Sales at
1-866-506-1949 or business@simonandschuster.com.

The Simon & Schuster Speakers Bureau can bring authors to your
live event. For more information or to book an event, contact the
Simon & Schuster Speakers Bureau at 1-866-248-3049 or visit our
website at www.simonspeakers.com.

Cover art by Marco Ventura

Manufactured in the United States of America

12   11   10   9   8   7   6   5   4   3

ISBN 978-1-4165-0037-7

CONTENTS

INTRODUCTION

Beowulf:
HARSH STRUGGLE AND QUIET GRACE

Beowulf is one of the world's great works of imaginative literature, set in early Christian England in the years before the end of the first millennium—a world of harsh cold, darkness, heroic warfare, minstrelsy, death, and struggle. *Beowulf* remains a timeless classic a thousand years after its birth because it both brings that old English history to life in our own era and resonates with the timeless quality of all great stories. At its opening, the epic transports us into a land of mystery where a lamented king has died. At the end of the poem the story comes full circle: we see that Beowulf, who was a young hero in the first half of the poem, as an aged hero, as deeply human as was the king whose death opens the epic. Between the beginning and the end, of course, are some truly incredible adventures filled with gore, guts, horror, and heroism.

Beowulf's beautifully poetic, tragic treatment of the themes of aging and wisdom secures its place among the world's masterpieces. But, of course, this is not merely a poem about aging but a prototypical hero story, filled with dramatic events and bloody struggles. The poem sustains its air of beautiful mystery, and its painful awareness of the struggling transience of human life, at a gripping level throughout the epic, whether we are pondering the solemnity of funeral rites or hunched in suspense in the middle of one of Beowulf's many exciting battles. This is true not only of the story itself, which moves from youth to age as our characters face an endless series of threats; it is also true at the level of the language—of the poetry itself. For *Beowulf* is filled with poetic language of great sophistication and beauty, so beautiful that it is audible even in its contemporary English translations. Reading these—and, perhaps, attempting the poem in its original language—we can see metrical, metaphoric, and stylistic subtleties that can only have flourished in a high civilization.

The civilization that produced *Beowulf* has deeply influenced our own. The heroic world of early Norse England, with its great halls, its dauntless seafarers, and its heroic codes of behavior, may seem very far removed from our own world. But this Anglo-Saxon culture formed the basis for the Northern European, Germanic, and, of course, English cultures that still live on in America today. The values codified in the Anglo-Saxon communities of the first millennium—honor, persistence, hard work, valor—have come to us through hundreds of years and countless generations and still inform our laws and lives today.

The Origins of *Beowulf*

No one knows who wrote *Beowulf*. The original manuscript may first have been written out shortly after the year 1000, and that date may have been a good three hundred years after the creation of the poem itself. Scholars have proposed dates ranging from 675 to the early twelfth century for the creation of the poem, based on criteria including the original inception of the poetic material, the first recitation of the material, or the point at which diverse strands of an oral tradition were stitched together. Adding to the uncertainty of this dating process is the fact that we do not know whether the poem *Beowulf* was a completely oral composition or was part written. If the author of the poem was a monk or other educated writer attached to an Anglo-Saxon monastery, which is one mainstream theory, we can push the date of composition of the poem much later than the year 700. If the author was a bard, a scop to the Norse, the creation of something like our present *Beowulf* may have occurred in the late seventh or early eighth century.

Historical and Literary Context of *Beowulf*

Manuscript and Publication

Beowulf survived the vicissitudes of history in a single manuscript belonging to the private collection of Sir Robert Cotton (1571–1631). After Cotton's collection was damaged by fire in 1731, *Beowulf* was moved to the British Museum, where it resides today. To look at this manuscript is to shiver with the realization that our cultural history is fragile: the margins of the text are visibly charred by the flames that so nearly deprived us entirely of this precious vestige of early English culture.

The first publicly available edition of *Beowulf* was published in 1815. Its first translation into modern English dates from 1837. Unlike *The Canterbury Tales* by Geoffrey Chaucer (c.1342–1400), *Beowulf* is a relatively recent part of the canon of English literature. Some scholars have linked the rising literary status of *Beowulf* to a British yearning for ancient national roots as its ever expanding empire brought it into contact with the powerful, and extremely old, civilizations of the East.

Language and Form

The first dimension of *Beowulf*'s literary history is its language. *Beowulf* was composed in Late West Saxon, the standard vernacular used for writing down Anglo-Saxon poetry. This is an early Germanic form of English, before it had blended with Latin and French in the course of the Norman invasions of the eleventh century. *Beowulf* is written in alliterative verse, in which each line is divided into two metrical halves, with two stressed syllables in each half. At least one, and usually both, of the stressed syllables in the first half line alliterate (have the same beginning sound) with the first stressed word of the second half line. Recited to the harp in a fashion often described in the poem of *Beowulf*, this poetry must have been powerful and mesmerizing. Throw in a roaring fire, fifty thanes chomping on boar meat, and the dark outside, and you have the ingredients for vigorous and decidedly premodern entertainment.

Placing Beowulf in History

Beowulf was composed by an Anglo-Saxon (or West Saxon) looking back to Scandinavian and North German lands from a distant pagan past. Therefore, we know that this epic is to some extent a reconstruction of the past. Though we do not know the precise date either of *Beowulf* the poem or of the historical events from which it is drawn, scholars have made a few broad guesses. *Beowulf* itself seems to have been composed in the late seventh or early eighth century, while historical and archaeological evidence suggests that the period portrayed in the poem may be as early as the sixth century AD. One of the most sensational examples of such evidence comes from Anglo-Saxon archaeology. The Sutton Hoo burial ship, discovered in Suffolk, England, in 1938–39, lays out for us the vestiges of a hero's burial: a brilliant spread of gold and silver artifacts, of military and nautical equipment, corresponding to much of the heroic paraphernalia assembled for funeral rites in the poem *Beowulf*. The date of the Sutton Hoo burial is AD 620–630, which *may* put it a century and a half or two before the composition of the poem of *Beowulf*.

The Rise of Europe and England

Beowulf is a product of the great historical developmental process that followed the breakdown of the Roman Empire in the West of Europe and led eventually to the establishment of the European nation states we know today. It lies at the beginning of this long historical transition, and is among the many literary documents that herald the development of what would become modern England.

By the early years of the fifth century AD, the Roman government of Britain had begun to collapse—as had the Roman hold on its entire empire. From archaeological and later chronicle evidence—such as that of Bede in his

Ecclesiastical History of the English People, completed about 732, or the *Anglo-Saxon Chronicle*, from the late ninth century—we know that during the fall of the Roman Empire, the British Isles were being colonized by Northern European tribes such as the Frisians, Danes, and Saxons. Slowly, and in the course of endless wars, these tribes mixed with the native Britons and Celts. A decisive event in this new colonization of the British Isles took place at the end of the sixth century, when Pope Gregory the Great sent Augustine from Rome to Kent, where he established Christ Church, a beacon for the now rapidly expanding Christian population of England. From that date begins the "modernizing" process of the British Isles, in which the many disparate cultures and religions that had flourished under Roman rule were gradually brought under the reign of the Church.

It was not long before the extraordinarily rich Anglo-Saxon poetic tradition began to flourish. This Old English poetry preserves for us a library of fine texts, including *Widsith, The Wanderer, The Seafarer*, and *The Battle of Maldon*, all of which emerge out of more or less the same temporal and literary crucible as *Beowulf*. In their pages we can sense the enormity and difficulty of historical, cultural, linguistic, and spiritual change under way as both the Christian and pagan worlds blend in a swirl of nostalgia, historical loneliness, and faith.

HISTORICAL CONTEXT OF
Beowulf

410: Roman troops leave the Roman province of Britain.

450–600: After departure of Roman forces from Britain, a prolonged incursion of Germanic tribes (Angles, Saxons, Frisians) into Britain, where they struggled with the local inhabitants, the Welsh and British.

521: Raid by Hygelac (uncle of Beowulf in *Beowulf*) on the continent; record of this in work of Gregory of Tours.

597: Augustine, sent by Pope Gregory the Great, takes over as archbishop of Canterbury and starts to convert the locals to Christianity.

650–660: Sutton Hoo ship burial site in East Anglia.

670–735: Lifetime of The Venerable Bede, Northumbrian writer of the *Ecclesiastical History of the English People*.

700: Approximated date of the composition of *Beowulf*.

c.732–804: Life of Alcuin of York, learned Christian

scholar who carried his teaching to the court of Charlemagne.

793: Destruction by Norsemen of the monastery at Lindisfarne; opening for many decades of invasions and depredations.

849–899: Life of King Alfred the Great of Wessex; did much to stop Norse incursions and to inspire cultural development in Britain.

991: Battle of Maldon, scene of English defeat by the Norse and topic of long Anglo-Saxon poem.

1000: Date of writing down of the manuscript of *Beowulf*.

1066: Victory of the Normans over the British at Hastings; end of the Anglo-Saxon age.

1571–1631: Life of Sir Robert Cotton, early owner of the manuscript of *Beowulf*.

1731: Manuscript of *Beowulf* survives fire and is moved to British Museum.

1815: First edition of *Beowulf* published.

BEOWULF

I

Lo! WE HAVE heard the glory of the kings of the Spear-Danes in days gone by, how the chieftains wrought mighty deeds. Often Scyld-Scefing[1] wrested the mead-benches from troops of foes, from many tribes; he made fear fall upon the earls. After he was first found in misery[2] (he received solace for that), he grew up under the heavens, lived in high honour, until each of his neighbours over the whale-road[3] must needs obey him and render tribute. That was a good king! Later a young son was born to him in the court, God sent him for a comfort to the people; He had marked the misery of that earlier time when they suffered long space, lacking a leader. Wherefore the Lord of life, the Ruler of glory, gave him honour in the world.

Beowulf,[4] son of Scyld, was renowned in Scandinavian lands—his repute spread far and wide. So shall a young man bring good to pass with splendid gifts in his father's possession, so that when war comes willing comrades shall stand by him again in his old age, the people follow him. In every tribe a man shall prosper by deeds of love.

Then at the fated hour Scyld, very brave, passed hence into the Lord's protection. Then did they, his dear comrades, bear him out to the shore of the sea, as he himself had besought them, whilst as friend of the Scyldings,[5] loved lord of the land, he held sway long time with speech. There at the haven stood the ring-prowed ship radiant and ready, the chieftain's vessel. Then they laid down the loved lord, the bestower of rings[6] on the bosom of the barge, the famous man by the mast. Many treasures and ornaments were there, brought from afar. I never heard of a sightlier ship adorned with weapons of war and garments of battle, swords and corslets. Many treasures lay on his bosom that were to pass far with him into the power of the flood. No whit less did they furnish him with gifts, with great costly stores, than did those who sent him forth in the beginning while he was still a child alone over the waves. Further they set a golden banner high over his head; they let the ocean bear him; they surrendered him to the sea. Sad was their mind, mournful their mood. Men cannot tell for a truth, counsellors in hall, heroes under the heavens, who received that burden.

II

Then beowulf of the Scyldings, beloved king of the people, was famed among warriors long time in the strongholds—his father had passed hence, the prince from his home—until noble Healfdene was born to him; aged and fierce in fight, he ruled the Scyldings graciously while he lived. Four children sprang from him in succession, Heorogar, prince of troops, and Hrothgar, and Halga the good; I heard that Sigeneow was Onela's[1] queen, consort of the war-Scylfing. Then good fortune in war was granted to Hrothgar, glory in battle, so that his kinsmen gladly obeyed him, until the younger warriors grew to be a mighty band.

It came into his mind that he would order men to make a hall-building, a mighty mead-dwelling, greater than ever the children of men had heard of; and therein that he should part among young and old all which God gave unto him except the nation and the lives of men.[2] Then I heard far and wide of work laid upon many a tribe throughout this world, the task of adorning the

place of assembly. Quickly it came to pass among men
that it was perfect; the greatest of hall-dwellings; he
whose word had wide sway gave it the name of Heorot.[3]
He broke not his pledge, he bestowed bracelets and trea-
sure at the banquet. The hall towered up, lofty and wide-
gabled; it endured the surges of battle, of hostile fire.
The time was not yet come when the feud between son-
in-law and father-in-law was fated to flare out after
deadly hostility.[4]

Then the mighty spirit[5] who dwelt in darkness angrily
endured the torment of hearing each day high revel in
the hall. There was the sound of the harp, the clear song
of the minstrel.[6] He who could tell of men's beginning
from olden times spoke of how the Almighty wrought the
world, the earth bright in its beauty which the water en-
compasses; the Victorious One established the brightness
of sun and moon for a light to dwellers in the land, and
adorned the face of the earth with branches and leaves;
He also created life of all kinds which move and live.
Thus the noble warriors lived in pleasure and plenty, until
a fiend in hell began to contrive malice. The grim spirit
was called Grendel, a famous march-stepper, who held
the moors, the fen and the fastness. The hapless creature
sojourned for a space in the sea-monsters' home after the
Creator had condemned him. The eternal Lord avenged
the murder on the race of Cain, because he slew Abel.
He did not rejoice in that feud. He, the Lord, drove him
far from mankind for that crime. Thence sprang all evil
spawn, ogres and elves and sea-monsters, giants too, who
struggled a long time against God. He paid them requital
for that.

III

HE WENT THEN when night fell to visit the high house, to see how the Ring-Danes had disposed themselves in it after the beer-banquet. Then he found therein the band of chieftains slumbering after the feast; they knew not sorrow, the misery of men, aught of misfortune. Straightway he was ready, grim and ravenous, savage and raging; and seized thirty thanes on their couches. Thence he departed homewards again, exulting in booty, to find out his dwelling with his fill of slaughter.

Then at dawn with the breaking of day the war-might of Grendel was made manifest to men; then after the feasting arose lamentation, a loud cry in the morning. The renowned ruler, the prince long famous, sat empty of joy; strong in might, he suffered, sorrowed for his men when they saw the track of the hateful monster, the evil spirit. That struggle was too hard, too hateful, and lasting. After no longer lapse than one night again he wrought still more murders, violence and malice, and mourned not for it; he was too bent on that. Then that man was easy to find who sought elsewhere for himself a more remote resting-place, a bed after the banquet, when the hate of the hall-visitant[1] was shown to him, truly declared by a plain token; after that he kept himself further off, and more securely. He escaped the fiend.

Thus one against all prevailed and pitted himself against right until the peerless house stood unpeopled. That was a weary while. For the space of twelve winters the friend of the Scyldings bitterly suffered every woe, deep sorrows; wherefore it came to be known to people, to the children of men, sadly in songs, that Grendel waged long war with Hrothgar; many years he bore bitter hatred, violence and malice, an unflagging feud; peace he would not have with any man of Danish race, nor lay aside murderous death, nor consent to be bought off.[2] Nor did any of the councillors make bold to expect fairer conditions from the hands of the slayer; but the monster, the deadly creature, was hostile to warriors young and old; he plotted and planned. Many nights he held the misty moors. Men do not know whither the demons go in their wanderings.

Thus the foe of men, the dread lone visitant, oftentimes wrought many works of malice, sore injuries; in the dark nights he dwelt in Heorot, the treasure-decked hall. He might not approach the throne, the precious thing, for fear of the Lord, nor did he know his purpose.[3]

That was heavy sorrow, misery of mind for the friend of the Scyldings. Many a mighty one sat often in council; they held debate what was best for bold-minded men to do against sudden terrors. Sometimes in their temples they vowed sacrifices, they petitioned with prayers that the slayer of souls[4] should succour them for the people's distress. Such was their wont, the hope of the heathen.

Their thoughts turned to hell; they knew not the Lord, the Judge of deeds; they wist not the Lord God; nor in truth could they praise the Protector of the heavens, the Ruler of glory. Woe is it for him who must needs send forth his soul in unholiness and fear into the embrace of the fire, hope for no solace, suffer no change! Well is it for him who may after the day of death seek the Lord, and crave shelter in the Father's embrace!

IV

Thus the son of Healfdene was ever troubled with care; nor could the sage hero sweep aside his sorrows. That struggle was too hard, too hateful and lasting, which fell on the people—fierce hostile oppression, greatest of night-woes.

Hygelac's thane,[1] a valiant man among the Geats, heard of that at home, of the deeds of Grendel. He was the greatest in might among men at that time, noble and powerful. He bade a good ship to be built for him; he said that he was set on seeking the warlike king, the famous prince over the swan-road,[2] since he had need of men. No whit did wise men blame him for the venture, though he was dear to them; they urged on the staunch-minded man, they watched the omens. The valiant man had chosen warriors of the men of the Geats, the boldest he could find; with fourteen others he sought the ship. A man cunning in knowledge of the sea led them to the shore.

Time passed on; the ship was on the waves, the boat

beneath the cliff. The warriors eagerly embarked. The currents turned the sea against the sand. Men bore bright ornaments, splendid war-trappings, to the bosom of the ship. The men, the heroes on their willing venture, shoved out the well-timbered ship. The foamy-necked floater like a bird went then over the wave-filled sea, sped by the wind, till after due time on the next day the boat with twisted prow had gone so far that the voyagers saw land, the sea-cliffs shining, the steep headlands, the broad sea-capes. Then the sea was traversed, the journey at an end. The men of the Weders mounted thence quickly to the land; they made fast the ship. The armour rattled, the garments of battle. They thanked God that the sea voyage had been easy for them.

Then the watchman of the Scyldings whose duty it was to guard the sea-cliffs saw from the height bright shields and battle-equipment ready for use borne over the gangway. A desire to know who the men were pressed on his thoughts. The thane of Hrothgar went to the shore riding his steed; mightily he brandished his spear in his hands, spoke forth a question: "What warriors are ye, clad in corslets, who have come thus bringing the high ship over the way of waters, hither over the floods? Lo! for a time I have been guardian of our coasts, I have kept watch by the sea lest any enemies should make ravage with their sea-raiders on the land of the Danes. No shield-bearing warriors have ventured here more openly; nor do ye know at all that ye have the permission of warriors, the consent of kinsmen. I never saw in the world a greater earl than one of your band is, a hero in his harness. He is no mere retainer decked out with weapons, unless

his face belies him, his excellent front. Now I must
know your race rather than ye should go further hence
and be thought spies in the land of the Danes. Now,
ye far-dwellers, travellers of the sea, hearken to my
frank thought. It is best to tell forth quickly whence ye
are come."

V

THE ELDEST ANSWERED him; the leader of the troop unlocked his word-hoard: "We are men of the race of the Geats and hearth-companions of Hygelac. My father was famed among the peoples, a noble high prince called Ecgtheow; he sojourned many winters ere he passed away, the old man from his dwelling. Far and wide throughout the earth every wise man remembers him well. We have come with gracious intent to seek out thy lord, the son of Healfdene, the protector of his people. Be kindly to us in counsel. We have a great errand to the famous prince of the Danes. Nor shall anything be hidden there, I hope. Thou knowest if the truth is, as indeed we heard tell, that some sort of foe, a secret pursuer, works on the dark nights evil hatred, injury and slaughter, spreading terror. I can give Hrothgar counsel from a generous mind, how he may overcome the enemy wisely and well, if for him the torment of ills should ever cease, relief come again, and the surges of care grow cooler; or if he shall ever after suffer a time of misery and pain while the best of houses stands there in its lofty station."

The watchman spoke, the fearless servant, where he sat his steed—a bold shield-warrior who ponders well shall pass judgment on both words and deeds: "I hear that this is a troop friendly to the prince of the Scyldings. Go forth and bear weapons and trappings; I will guide you. Likewise I will bid my henchmen honourably guard your vessel against all enemies, your newly-tarred ship on the sand, until once more the boat with twisted prow shall bear the beloved man to the coast of the Weders; to such a valiant one it shall be vouchsafed to escape unscathed from the rush of battle."

They went on their way then. The ship remained at rest; the broad-bosomed vessel was bound by a rope, fast at anchor. The boar-images[1] shone over the cheek armour, decked with gold; gay with colour and hardened by fire they gave protection to the brave men. The warriors hastened, went up together, until they could see the well-built hall, splendid and gold-adorned. That was foremost of buildings under the heavens for men of the earth, in which the mighty one dwelt; the light shone over many lands.

The man bold in battle pointed out to them the abode of brave men, as it gleamed, so that they could go thither. One of the warriors turned his horse, then spoke a word: "It is time for me to go. The almighty Father guard you by his grace safe in your venture. I will to the sea to keep watch for a hostile horde."

VI

T HE STREET WAS paved with stones of various colours,
the road kept the warriors together. The war-corslet
shone, firmly hand-locked, the gleaming iron rings sang
in the armour as they came on their way in their trap-
pings of war even to the hall. Weary from the sea, they
set down their broad shields, their stout targes against
the wall of the building; they sat down on the bench
then. The corslets rang out, the warriors' armour. The
spears, the weapons of seamen, of ash wood grey at the
tip, stood all together. The armed band was adorned with
war-gear. Then a haughty hero[1] asked the men of battle
as to their lineage: "Whence bear ye plated shields, grey
corslets and masking helmets, this pile of spears? I am
Hrothgar's messenger and herald. I have not seen so
many men of strange race more brave in bearing. I sup-
pose ye have sought Hrothgar from pride, by no means
as exiles but with high minds."

The bold man, proud prince of the Weders, answered
him, spoke a word in reply, stern under his helmet: "We

are Hygelac's table-companions; Beowulf is my name. I wish to tell my errand to the son of Healfdene, the famous prince, thy lord, if he will grant that we may greet him who is so gracious." Wulfgar spoke—he was a man of the Wendels; his courage, his bravery and his wisdom had been made known to many: "I will ask the friend of the Danes, the prince of the Scyldings, the giver of rings, the renowned ruler, about thy venture as thou desirest, and speedily make known to thee the answer which the gracious one thinks fit to give me." He turned quickly then to where Hrothgar sat, aged and grey-haired, amid the band of earls; the bold man went till he stood before the shoulders of the Danish prince; he knew courtly custom. Wulfgar spoke to his gracious master: "Men of the Geats, come from afar, have been brought here over the stretch of the ocean. The warriors call the eldest one Beowulf. They request, my lord, that they may exchange words with thee. Refuse them not thy answer, gracious Hrothgar. They seem in their war-gear worthy of respect from the noble-born. Of a truth the leader is valiant who guided the heroes hither."

VII

HROTHGAR SPOKE, THE protector of the Scyldings: "I knew him when he was a youth. His aged father was called Ecgtheow; to him Hrethel of the Geats[1] gave his only daughter in marriage. His son has now come here boldly, has sought a gracious friend. Then seafaring men, who brought precious gifts of the Geats hither as a present, said that he, mighty in battle, had the strength of thirty men in the grip of his hand. May Holy God in his graciousness send him to us, to the West-Danes, as I hope, against the terror of Grendel. I shall offer treasures to the valiant one for his courage. Do thou hasten, bid them enter to see the friendly band all together; tell them also with words that they are welcome to the people of the Danes." Then Wulfgar went toward the door of the hall, spoke a word in the doorway: "My victorious lord, prince of the East-Danes, bade me tell you that he knows your lineage, and that ye, bold in mind, are welcome hither over the sea-surges. Now ye may go in your war-gear under battle-helmets to see Hrothgar; let your battle-shields, spears, deadly shafts, await here the issue of the speaking."

The mighty one rose then, around him many a warrior, excellent troop of thanes. Some waited there, kept watch over their trappings, as the bold man bade them. They hastened together, as the warrior guided, under the roof of Heorot; the man, resolute in mind, stern under his helmet, went till he stood within the hall. Beowulf spoke—on him his corslet shone, the shirt of mail sewn by the art of the smith: "Hail to thee, Hrothgar; I am Hygelac's kinsman and thane. I have in my youth undertaken many heroic deeds. The ravages of Grendel were made known to me in my native land. Seafarers say that this hall, the noblest building, stands unpeopled and profitless to all warriors, after the light of evening is hidden under cover of heaven. Then my people counselled me, the best of men in their wisdom, that I should seek thee, Prince Hrothgar, because they knew the power of my strength, they saw it themselves, when I came out of battles, blood-stained from my foes, where I bound five, ruined the race of the monsters and slew by night the sea-beasts mid the waves, suffered sore need, avenged the wrong of the Weders, killed the foes—they embarked on an unlucky venture. And now alone I shall achieve the exploit against Grendel, the monster, the giant. I wish now at this time to ask thee one boon, prince of the Bright-Danes,[2] protector of the Scyldings: that thou, defence of warriors, friendly prince of the people, wilt not refuse me, now I have come thus far, that I and my band of earls, this bold troop, may cleanse Heorot unaided. I have also heard that the monster in his madness cares naught for weapons; wherefore I scorn to bear sword or broad shield, yellow targe to the battle,

so may Hygelac my lord be gracious in mind to me; but
with my grip I shall seize the fiend and strive for his life,
foe against foe. There he whom death takes must needs
trust to the judging of the Lord. I think that he is
minded, if he can bring it to pass, to devour fearlessly in
the battle-hall the people of the Geats, the flower of
men, as he often has done. Not at all dost thou need to
protect my head,[3] but if death takes me he will have me
drenched in blood; he will carry off the bloody corpse,
will think to hide it; the lone-goer will feed without
mourning, he will stain the moor-refuges. No longer
needst thou care about the sustenance of my body. Send
to Hygelac, if battle takes me off, the best of battle-
garments that arms my breast, the finest of corslets. That
is a heritage from Hrethel, the work of Weland.[4] Fate
ever goes as it must."

VIII

HROTHGAR SPOKE, THE protector of the Scyldings: "Thou hast sought us, my friend Beowulf, for battle and from graciousness. Thy father achieved the greatest of feuds; he became the slayer of Heatholaf among the Wulfings; then the race of the Weders would not receive him because of threatening war. Thence he sought the people of the South-Danes, the honourable Scyldings, over the surging of the waves. Then I had just begun to rule the Danish people and in youth held a wide-stretched kingdom, a stronghold of heroes. Then Heregar was dead, my elder kinsman, the son of Healfdene had ceased to live; he was better than I. Afterwards I ended the feud with money; I sent old treasures to the Wulfings over the back of the water; he[1] swore oaths to me. It is sorrow for me in my mind to tell any man what malice and sudden onslaughts Grendel has wrought on Heorot with his hostile thoughts. Thinned is my troop in hall, my war-band. Fate has swept them away to the dread Grendel. God may easily part the bold enemy from his deeds.

20

"Full often did warriors drunken with beer boast over the ale-cup that they would await Grendel's attack with dread blades in the beer-hall. Then in the morning, when day dawned, this mead-hall, the troop-hall, was stained with blood; all the ale-benches drenched with gore, the hall with blood shed in battle. I had so many the less trusty men, dear veterans, since death had carried off these. Sit down now at the banquet, and speak thy mind, tell the men of victorious fame, as thy mind prompts."

Then a bench was cleared in the beer-hall for the men of the Geats together; there the bold-minded ones went and sat down, exceeding proud. A thane who bore in his hands the decked ale-cup performed the office, poured out the gleaming beer. At times the minstrel sang clearly in Heorot; there was joy of heroes, a great band of warriors, Danes and Weders.

IX

UNFERTH SPOKE, SON of Ecglaf, who sat at the feet of the prince of the Scyldings. He began dispute—the journey of Beowulf, the brave seafarer, was a great bitterness to him, because he did not grant that any other man in the world accomplished greater exploits under heaven than he himself: "Art thou that Beowulf who strove with Breca, contended on the wide sea for the prize in swimming, where ye two tried the floods in your pride, and risked your lives in the deep water from presumption? Nor could any man, friend or foe, prevent the sorrowful journey; then ye two swam on the sea, where ye plied the ocean-streams with your arms, measured the sea-paths, threw aside the sea with your hands, glided over the surge; the deep raged with its waves, with its wintry flood. Seven nights ye toiled in the power of the water; he outstripped thee in swimming, had greater strength. Then in the morning the sea bore him to the land of the Heathoremes. Thence, dear to his people, he sought his loved country, the land of the Brondings, the fair stronghold, where he ruled over people, castle and rings. The son of Beanstan in truth fulfilled all his pledge to thee. Wherefore I expect a worse fate for thee, though everywhere thou hast withstood battle-rushes, grim war, if thou durst await Grendel throughout the night near at hand."

Beowulf spoke, son of Ecgtheow: "Lo! thou hast spoken a great deal, friend Unferth, about Breca, drunken as thou art with beer; thou hast told of his journey. I count it as truth that I had greater might in the sea, hardships mid the waves, than any other man.

"We arranged that and made bold, while we were youths—we were both then still in our boyhood—that we two should risk our lives out on the sea; and thus we accomplished that. We held naked swords boldly in our hands when we swam in the ocean; we thought to protect ourselves against the whales. In no wise could he swim far from me on the waves of the flood, more quickly on the sea; I would not consent to leave him. Then we were together on the sea for the space of five nights till the flood forced us apart, the surging sea, coldest of storms, darkening night, and a wind from the north, battle-grim, came against us. Wild were the waves; the temper of the sea-monsters was stirred. There did my shirt of mail hard-locked by hand stand me in good stead against foes; the woven battle-garment, adorned with gold, lay on my breast. A spotted deadly foe drew me to the depths, had me firmly and fiercely in his grip; yet it was granted to me that I pierced the monster with my point, my battle-spear. The rush of battle carried off the mighty sea-monster by my hand.

X

"THUS OFTENTIMES MALICIOUS foes pressed me hard. I served them with my good sword, as was fitting. They had not joy of their feasting, the evildoers, from devouring me, from sitting round the banquet near the bottom of the sea; but in the morning they lay cast up on the shore, wounded with swords, laid low by blades, so that no longer they hindered seafarers on their voyage over the high flood. Light came from the east, bright beacon of God. The surges sank down, so that I could behold the sea-capes, the windy headlands. Fate often succours the undoomed warrior when his valour is strong.

"Yet it was my fortune to slay with the sword nine sea-monsters. I have not heard under the arching sky of heaven of harder fighting by night, nor of a more hapless man in the streams of ocean. Yet I escaped with my life from the grasp of foes, weary of travel. Then the sea, the flood, the raging surges bore me to the shore in the land of the Finns.

"I have not heard such exploits told of thee, dread

deeds, terror of swords; never yet did Breca or either of you two in the play of battle perform so bold a deed with gleaming blades—I do not boast of the struggle—though thou camest to be the murderer of thy brother, thy near kinsman. For that thou must needs suffer damnation in hell, though thy wit is strong. Forsooth, I tell thee, son of Ecglaf, that Grendel, the fearful monster, had never achieved so many dread deeds against thy prince, malice on Heorot, if thy thoughts and mind had been as daring as thou thyself sayest. But he has found out that he need not sorely dread the feud, the terrible sword-battle of your people, the victorious Scyldings; he takes pledges by force, he spares none of the Danish people, but he lives in pleasure, sleeps and feasts; he looks for no fight from the Spear-Danes. But soon now I shall show him battle, the might and courage of the Geats. He who may will go afterwards, brave to the mead, when the morning light of another day, the sun clothed with sky-like brightness, shines from the south over the children of men."

Then glad was the giver of treasure, grey-haired and famed in battle; the prince of the Bright-Danes trusted in aid; the protector of the people heard in Beowulf a resolute purpose. There was laughter of heroes; talk was heard; words were winsome.

Wealtheow went forth, Hrothgar's queen, mindful of what was fitting; gold-adorned, she greeted the warriors in hall; and the free-born woman first offered the goblet to the guardian of the East-Danes; bade him be of good cheer at the beer-banquet, be dear to his people. He gladly took part in the banquet and received the hall-goblet, the king mighty in victory. Then the woman of the Helmings went about everywhere among old and young warriors, proffered the precious cup, till the time came that she, the ring-decked queen, excellent in mind, bore the mead-flagon to Beowulf. She greeted the prince of the Geats, thanked God with words of sober wisdom that her wish had been fulfilled, that she might trust to some earl as a comfort in trouble. He, the warrior fierce in fight, took that goblet from Wealtheow, and then, ready for battle, uttered speech.

Beowulf spoke, son of Ecgtheow: "That was my purpose when I launched on the ocean, embarked on the sea-boat with the band of my warriors, that I should work the will of your people to the full, or fall a corpse fast in the foe's grip. I shall accomplish deeds of heroic might, or endure my last day in the mead-hall."

Those words, the boasting speech of the Geat, pleased the woman well. Decked with gold, the free-born queen of the people went to sit by her prince. Then again as before there was excellent converse in hall, the warriors in happiness, the sound of victorious people, till all at once Healfdene's son was minded to seek his evening's rest. He knew that war was destined to the high hall by the monster after they could no longer see the light of the sun, and when, night growing dark over all, the shadowy creatures came stalking, black beneath the clouds. The troop all rose.

Then one warrior greeted the other, Hrothgar Beowulf, and wished him success, power over the wine-hall, and spoke these words: "Never before did I trust to any man, since I was able to lift hand and shield, the excellent hall of the Danes, except to thee now. Have now and hold the best of houses. Be mindful of fame, show a mighty courage, watch against foes. Nor shalt thou lack what thou desirest, if with thy life thou comest out from that heroic task."

XI

Then hrothgar went his way with his band of heroes, the protector of Scyldings out of the hall; the warlike king was minded to seek Wealtheow the queen for his bedfellow. The glorious king had, as men learned, set a hall-guardian against Grendel; he performed a special service for the prince of the Danes, kept watch against monsters. Truly the prince of the Geats relied firmly on his fearless might, and the grace of the Lord. Then he laid aside his iron corslet, the helmet from his head, gave his ornamented sword, best of blades, to his servant and bade him keep his war-gear.

Then the valiant one, Beowulf of the Geats, spoke some words of boasting ere he lay down on his bed: "I do not count myself less in war-strength, in battle-deeds, than Grendel does himself; wherefore I will not slay him, spoil him of life by sword, although I might. He knows not the use of weapons so as to strike at me, hew my shield, though he may be mighty in works of malice; but we two shall do without swords in the night, if he dare to seek war without weapons, and afterwards the wise God, the holy Lord, shall award fame to whatever side seems good to Him." The bold warrior lay down, the earl's face touched the bolster; and round him many a mighty sea-hero bent to his couch in the hall. None of them thought that he should go thence and seek again the loved land, the people or stronghold where he was fostered; but they had heard that murderous death had ere now carried off far too many of Danish people in the wine-hall. But the Lord gave them success in war, support and succour to the men of the Weders, so that through the strength of one, his own might, they all overcame their foe. The truth has been made known, that mighty God has ever ruled over mankind.

The shadowy visitant came stalking in the dark night. The warriors slept, who were to keep the antlered building, all save one. That was known to men that the ghostly enemy might not sweep them off among the shadows, for the Lord willed it not; but he, watching in anger against foes, awaited in wrathful mood the issue of the battle.

XII

THEN FROM THE moor under the misty cliffs came Grendel, he bore God's anger. The foul foe purposed to trap with cunning one of the men in the high hall;[1] he went under the clouds till he might see most clearly the wine-building, the gold-hall of warriors, gleaming with plates of gold. That was not the first time he had sought Hrothgar's home; never in his life-days before or since did he find bolder heroes and hall-thanes. The creature came, bereft of joys, making his way to the building. Straightway the door, firm clasped by fire-hardened fetters, opened, when he touched it with his hands; then, pondering evil, he tore open the entry of the hall when he was enraged. Quickly after that the fiend trod the gleaming floor, moved angry in mood. A baleful light like flame flared from his eyes. He saw in the building many heroes, the troop of kinsmen sleeping together, the band of young warriors. Then his mind exulted. The dread monster purposed ere day came to part the life of each one from the body, for the hope of a great feasting filled him. No longer did fate will that after that night he might seize more of mankind. The kinsman of Hygelac, exceeding strong, beheld how the foul foe was minded to act with his sudden grips.

Nor did the monster think to delay, but first he quickly seized a sleeping warrior; suddenly tore him asunder, devoured his body, drank the blood from his veins, swallowed him with large bites. Straightway he had consumed all the body, even the feet and hands. He stepped forward nearer, laid hold with his hands of the resolute warrior on his couch; the fiend stretched his hand towards him. Beowulf met the attack quickly and propped himself on his arm. Forthwith the upholder of crime found that he had not met in the world, on the face of the earth among other men, a mightier hand-grip. Fear grew in his mind and heart; yet in spite of that he could not make off. He sought to move out; he was minded to flee to his refuge, to seek the troop of devils. His task there was not such as he had found in former days.

Then the brave kinsman of Hygelac remembered his speech in the evening; he stood upright and seized him firmly. The fingers burst, the monster was moving out; the earl stepped forward. The famous one purposed to flee further, if only he might, and win away thence to the fen-strongholds; he knew the might of his fingers was in the grip of his foe. That was an ill journey when the ravager came to Heorot. The warriors' hall resounded. Terror fell on all the Danes, on the castle-dwellers, on each of the bold men, on the earls. Wroth were they both, angry contestants for the house. The building rang aloud.

Then was it great wonder that the wine-hall withstood the bold fighters; that it fell not to the ground, the fair earth-dwelling; but it was too firmly braced within and without with iron bands of skilled workmanship. There many a mead-bench decked with gold bent away from the post, as I have heard, where the foemen fought. The wise men of the Scyldings looked not for that before, that any man could ever shatter it, rend it with malice in any way, excellent and bone-adorned as it was, unless the embrace of fire could swallow it in smoke. A sound arose, passing strange. Dread fear came upon each of the North-Danes who heard the cry from the wall, the lament of God's foe rise, the song of defeat; the hell-bound creature, crying out in his pain. He who was strongest in might among men at that time held him too closely.

XIII

THE PROTECTOR OF earls was minded in no wise to release the deadly visitant alive, nor did he count his life as useful to any man.

There most eagerly this one and that of Beowulf's men brandished old swords, wished to save their leader's life, the famous prince, if only they could. They did not know, when they were in the midst of the struggle, the stern warriors, and wished to strike on all sides, how to seek Grendel's life. No choicest of swords on the earth, no war-spear, would pierce the evil monster; but Beowulf had given up victorious weapons, all swords. His parting from life at that time was doomed to be wretched, and the alien spirit was to travel far into the power of the fiends.

Then he who before in the joy of his heart had wrought much malice on mankind—he was hostile to God—found that his body would not follow him, for the brave kinsman of Hygelac held him by the hand. Each was hateful to the other while he lived. The foul monster suffered pain in his body. A great wound was seen in his shoulder, the sinews sprang apart, the body burst open. Fame in war was granted to Beowulf. Grendel must needs flee thence under the fen-cliffs mortally wounded, seek out his joyless dwelling. He knew but too well the end of his life was come, the full count of his days. The desire of all the Danes was fulfilled after the storm of battle.

Then he who erstwhile came from afar, shrewd and staunch, had cleansed the hall of Hrothgar, freed it from battle. He rejoiced in the night-work, in heroic deeds. The prince of the Geat warriors had fulfilled his boast to the East-Danes; likewise he cured all their sorrows, sufferings from malicious foes, which they endured before and were forced to bear in distress, no slight wrong. That was a clear token when the bold warrior laid down the hand, the arm and shoulder under the wide roof—it was all there together—the claw of Grendel.

XIV

THEN IN THE morning, as I have heard, around the gift-hall was many a warrior; leaders came from far and near throughout the wide ways to behold the wonder, the tracks of the monster. His going from life did not seem grievous to any man who saw the course of the inglorious one, how, weary in mind, beaten in battle, fated and fugitive, he left behind him on his way thence to the mere[1] of the monsters marks of his life-blood. Then the water was surging with blood, the foul welter of waves all mingled with hot gore; it boiled with the blood of battle. The death-doomed one dived in, then bereft of joy in his fen-refuge he laid down his life, his heathen soul, when hell received him. Thence again old comrades went, also many a young man, in merry companionship, the brave men riding on horses from the mere, warriors on bay steeds. There Beowulf's fame was proclaimed. Oftentimes many a one said that neither south nor north between the seas, over the wide earth, under the vault of the sky, was there any better among warriors, more worthy of a kingdom. Nor in truth did they blame their friendly lord, gracious Hrothgar, for that was a good king.

At times the men doughty in battle let their sorrel horses run, race against one another, where the land-ways seemed fair to them, known for their good qualities; at times the kings thane, a man with many tales of exploits, mindful of measures, he who remembered a great number of the old legends, made a new story of things that were true. The man began again wisely to frame Beowulf's exploit and skilfully to make deft measures, to deal in words. He spoke all that he had heard told of Sigemund's mighty deeds, much that was unknown, the warfare of the son of Wæls,[2] the far journeys, the hostility and malice of which the children of men knew not at all, except Fitela who was with him when he was minded to say somewhat of such things, the uncle to his nephew; for they were always in every struggle bound together by kinship. They had felled with their swords very many of the race of giants. There sprang up for Sigemund after his death no little fame when the man bold in battle killed the dragon, the guardian of the treasure. Under the grey stone he ventured alone, the son of a chieftain, on the daring deed; Fitela was not with him. Yet it was granted to him that that sword pierced the monstrous dragon, so that it stood in the wall, the noble blade. The dragon died violently. The hero had brought it to pass by his valour that he could use the ring-hoard as he chose. The son of Wæls loaded the sea-boat, bore to the ship's bosom the bright ornaments. The dragon melted in heat.

He was by far the most famous of adventurers among men, protector of warriors by mighty deeds; he prospered by that earlier, when the boldness, the strength and the courage of Heremod[3] lessened. He was betrayed among the Eotens into the power of his enemies, quickly driven out. Surges of sorrow pressed him too long; he became a deadly grief to his people, to all his chieftains. So also many a wise man who trusted to him as a remedy for evils lamented in former times the valiant one's journey, that the prince's son was destined to prosper, inherit his father's rank, rule over the people, the treasure and the prince's fortress, the kingdom of heroes, the land of the Scyldings. There did he, the kinsman of Hygelac, become dearer to all men and to his friends than he. Treachery came upon him.

At times in rivalry they measured the yellow streets with their horses. Then the light of morning had quickly mounted up. Many a retainer went bold-minded to the high hall to behold the rare wonder; the king himself also, the keeper of ring-treasures, came glorious from his wife's chamber, famed for his virtues, with a great troop, and his queen with him measured the path to the mead-hall with a band of maidens.

XV

H ROTHGAR SPOKE—he went to the hall, stood on the doorstep, looked on the lofty gold-plated roof and Grendel's hand—"For this sight thanks be straightway rendered to the Almighty. I suffered much that was hateful, sorrows at the hands of Grendel; ever may God, the glorious Protector, perform wonder after wonder.

"That was not long since when I looked not ever to find solace for any of my woes, when the best of houses stood blood-stained, gory from battle; woe wide-spread among all councillors who had no hope of ever protecting the fortress of warriors against foes, against demons and evil spirits. Now the warrior has performed the deed through the Lord's might which formerly all of us could not contrive with our cunning. Lo! a woman who has borne such a son among the peoples, if she yet lives, may say that the ancient Lord was gracious to her in the birth of her son. Now I will love thee in my heart as my son, Beowulf, best of men; keep well the new kinship. Thou shalt lack none of the things thou desirest in the world, which I can command. Full often have I for less cause bestowed reward on a slighter warrior, a weaker in combat, to honour him with treasures. Thou hast brought it to pass for thyself by deeds that thy glory shall live forever. The All-Ruler reward thee with good things as He has done till now."

Beowulf spoke, son of Ecgtheow: "We accomplished that heroic deed, that battle, through great favour. We risked ourselves boldly against the might of the monster. I had rather that thou couldst have seen him, the fiend in his trappings, weary unto death. I thought to bind him speedily with strong clasps on his death-bed, so that he must needs lie in his death-agony by my hand-grip, unless his body should slip away. I could not, since the Lord willed it not, prevent his passing out. I did not hold him closely enough, the deadly enemy; the foe was too mighty in going. Nevertheless he left his hand, arm and shoulder, to serve as a token of his flight. Yet the wretched creature won no solace there; no longer lives the malicious foe pressed by sins, but pain has embraced him closely with hostile grasp, with ruinous bonds. There the creature stained with sin must needs await the great doom, what judgment the bright Lord will award him."

Then the son of Ecglaf[1] was a more silent man in boasting of war-deeds, when the chieftains beheld by the strength of the earl the hand, the fingers of the monster, stretching up to the high roof; each at its tip, each place where the nails were, was like steel, the heathen's claw, the monstrous spike of the fighter. Everyone said that no well-tried sword of brave men would wound him, would shorten the monster's bloody battle-fist.

XVI

THEN IT WAS quickly commanded that Heorot should be decked within with hands. There were many there, men and women, who made ready the wine-building, the guest-hall. Woven hangings gleamed, gold-adorned, on the walls, many wondrous sights for all men who look on such things. That bright building was all sorely shattered, though firm within with its iron clasps; its door-hinges burst. The roof alone survived all scathe-less, when the monster stained with evil deeds turned in flight, despairing of life. That is not easy to avoid—let him do it who will—but he must needs seek the place forced on him by necessity, prepared for all who bear souls, for the children of men, for the dwellers on earth, where his body sleeps after the banquet fast in its narrow bed.

Then was the time convenient and fitting that Healf-dene's son should go to the hall; the king himself wished to join in the banquet. I have not heard of a people who showed a nobler bearing with a greater troop about their

giver of treasure. The famous ones then sat down on the
bench, rejoiced in the feast; in seemly fashion they took
many a mead-goblet; brave-minded kinsmen were in the
high hall, Hrothgar and Hrothulf. Heorot within was
filled with friends. Not yet at this time had the Scyldings
practised treachery.[1]

The son of Healfdene gave then to Beowulf a golden
ensign as a reward for victory, an ornamented banner
with a handle, a helmet and corslet, a famous precious
sword. Many saw them borne before the warrior. Be-
owulf took the goblet in hall; he needed not to be
ashamed in front of the warriors of the bestowing of
gifts.

I have not heard of many men giving to others on the
ale-bench in more friendly fashion four treasures decked
with gold. Around the top of the helmet a jutting ridge
twisted with wires held guard over the head, so that
many an old sword, proved hard in battle, could not in-
jure the bold man, when the shield-bearing warrior was
destined to go against foes. Then the protector of earls
commanded eight horses with gold-plated bridles to be
led into the hall, into the house; on one of them lay a sad-
dle artfully adorned with gold, decked with costly orna-
ment. That was the war-seat of the noble king, when the
son of Healfdene was minded to practise sword-play.
Never did the bravery of the far-famed man fail in the
van when corpses were falling. Then the protector of the
friends of Ing[2] gave power over both to Beowulf, over
horses and weapons; he bade him use them well. Thus
manfully did the famous prince, the treasure-keeper of
heroes, reward the rushes of battle with steeds and rich
stores, so that he who wishes to speak truth in seemly
fashion will never scoff at them.

XVII

FURTHER THE LORD of earls bestowed treasure on the mead-bench, ancient blades, to each of those who travelled the ocean path with Beowulf; and he bade recompense to be made with gold for the one whom Grendel before murderously killed. So he was minded to do with more of them, if wise God and the man's courage had not turned aside such a fate from them. The Lord ruled over all mankind as He still does. Wherefore understanding, forethought of soul, is everywhere best. He who sojourns long in the world in these days of sorrow must needs suffer much of weal and woe.

There was song and music mingled before Healf-dene's chieftain; the harp was touched; a measure often recited at such times as it fell to Hrothgar's minstrel to proclaim joy in hall along the mead-bench. Hnæf of the Scyldings, a hero of the Half-Danes, was fated to fall in the Frisian battle-field when the sudden onslaught came upon them, the sons of Finn.[1] "Nor in truth had Hilde-burh[2] cause to praise the faith of the Eotens; sinless, she

was spoiled of her dear ones at the shield-play, a son and
a brother; wounded with the spear, they fell in succes-
sion. She was a sorrowing woman. Not without cause did
the daughter of Hoc lament her fate, when morning
came when she might see the slaughter of kinsmen
under the sky. Where erstwhile he had had greatest joy
in the world, war carried off all the thanes of Finn except
a very few, so that in no wise could he offer fight to
Hengest in the battle-field, nor protect by war the sad
survivors from the prince's thane; but they offered them
conditions,[3] that they would give up to them entirely an-
other building, the hall and high seat; that they might
have power over half of it with the men of the Eotens,
and that the son of Folcwalda[4] would honour the Danes
each day with gifts at the bestowal of presents, would pay
respect to Hengest's troop with rings, just as much as he
would encourage the race of the Frisians in the beer-hall
with ornaments of plated gold. Then on both sides they
had faith in firm-knit peace. Finn swore to Hengest
deeply, inviolably with oaths, that he would treat the sad
survivors honourably according to the judgment of the
councillors, that no man there should break the bond by
word or deed, nor should they ever mention it in malice,
although they had followed the slayer of their giver of
rings after they had lost their leader, since the necessity
was laid upon them; if then any one of the Frisians
should recall to mind by dangerous speech the deadly
hostility, then it must needs recall also the edge of the
sword.

"The oath was sworn and rich gold taken from the
treasure. The best of the heroes of the warlike Scyldings[5]
was ready on the funeral fire. On that pyre the blood-
stained shirt of mail was plain to see, the swine-image all

gold, the boar hard as iron, many a chieftain slain with wounds. Many had fallen in the fight. Then Hildeburh bade her own son to be given over to the flames at Hnæf's pyre, his body to be burned and placed on the funeral fire. The woman wept, sorrowing by his side; she lamented in measures. The warrior mounted up.[6] The greatest of funeral fires wound up to the clouds, it roared in front of the mound. Heads melted, wounds burst open, while blood gushed forth from the gashes in the bodies. The fire, greediest of spirits, consumed all those of both peoples whom war carried off there. Their mightiest men had departed.

XVIII

"THE WARRIORS WENT then, bereft of friends, to visit the dwellings, to see the land of the Frisians, the homes and the stronghold.[1] Then Hengest dwelt yet in peace with Finn for a winter stained with the blood of the slain; he thought of his land though he could not drive the ring-prowed ship on the sea (the ocean surged with storm, rose up against the wind; winter bound the waves with fetters of ice), till another year came into the dwellings; as those still do now who ever await an opportunity, the bright clear weather. Then winter was past; the bosom of the earth was fair; the exile purposed to depart, the guest out of the castle; he thought rather of vengeance for sorrow than of the sea journey, if he could bring the battle to pass in which he thought to take vengeance on the children of the Eotens. So he let things take their course when Hunlafing[2] laid in his bosom the gleaming sword, best of blades. Its edges were famed among the Eotens. Even so did deadly death by the sword come upon brave Finn in his own home, when

Guthlaf and Oslaf after their sea journey sorrowfully lamented the grim attack; they were wroth at their manifold woes; their restless spirit could not be ruled in their breast. Then was the hall reddened with corpses of foes, Finn slain likewise, the king mid his troop, and the queen taken. The warriors of the Scyldings bore to the ships all the house-treasure of the king of the land, whatever they could find at Finn's home of ornaments and jewels. They bore away on the sea voyage the noble woman to the Danes, led her to her people."

The song was sung, the glee-man's measure. Joy rose again, bench-music rang out clear, servants gave out wine from wondrous goblets. Then Wealtheow, under her golden circlet, came forth where the two valiant ones were sitting, uncle and nephew. At that time there was peace yet between them, each true to the other. Likewise Unferth sat there as a squire at the feet of the prince of the Scyldings. Each of them trusted his heart, that he had a noble mind, though he had not been faithful to his kinsmen at the play of swords. Then spoke the queen of the Scyldings: "Receive this goblet, my prince, giver of treasure. Rejoice, gold-friend of warriors, and speak to the Geats with kindly words,[3] as it is fitting to do. Be gracious to the Geats, mindful of gifts; far and near now thou hast peace. They said that thou wast minded to take the warrior for son. Heorot is cleansed, the bright ring-hall; be generous with many rewards while thou mayst, and leave to thy kinsmen subjects and kingdom, when thou must needs go forth to face thy destiny. I know my gracious Hrothulf, that he will treat the young men honourably, if thou, friend of the Scyldings, pass from the world before him. I think that he will richly reward our children, if he forgets not all the

favours we formerly showed him for his pleasure and ho-
nour, while he was still a child."

She turned then towards the bench where her sons
were, Hrethric and Hrothmund, and the sons of heroes,
the young men together; there the valiant one, Beowulf
of the Geats, sat by the two brothers.

XIX

To HIM WAS the flagon borne and a friendly invitation offered with words and the twisted gold vessel graciously presented; two bracelets, a corslet and rings, greatest of necklaces, of those which I have heard of on earth.

I have not heard of a better treasure-hoard of heroes under the sky since Hama carried off to the gleaming castle the necklace of the Brosings,[1] the trinket and treasure; he fled the malicious hostility of Eormenric; he chose everlasting gain. Hygelac of the Geats, grandson of Swerting, had the ring[2] on his last expedition, when beneath his banner he defended the treasure, guarded the booty of battle. Fate took him off, when in his pride he suffered misfortune in fight against the Frisians; the mighty prince bore the ornament, the precious stones over the sea; he fell under his shield. Then the king's body passed into the power of the Franks, his breast-garments and the ring also; less noble warriors stripped the bodies of the men of the Geats after the carnage of war; their bodies covered the battle-field. The hall rang with shouts of approval.

Wealtheow spoke, she uttered words before the troop: "Enjoy this ring happily, dear young Beowulf; and use this corslet, the great treasures, and prosper exceedingly; make thyself known mightily, and be to these youths kindly in counsel. I will not forget thy reward for that. Thou hast brought it about that far and near men ever praise thee, even as far as the sea hems in the home of the winds, the headlands. Blessed be thou while thou livest, nobly-born man. I will grant thee many treasures. Be thou gracious in deeds to my son, thou who art now in happiness. Here each earl is true to the other, gentle in mind, loyal to the lord. The thanes are willing, the people all ready, noble warriors after drinking. Do as I bid."

She went then to the seat. There was the choicest of banquets; the men drank wine; they knew not fate, dread destiny, as it had been dealt out to many of the earls. Afterwards came evening, and Hrothgar went to his chamber, the mighty one to his couch. A great band of earls occupied the hall, as they often did before; they cleared away bench-boards; it was spread over with beds and bolsters. One of the revellers, ready and fated, sank to his couch in the hall. At their heads they placed the war-shields, the bright bucklers. There on the bench was plainly seen above the chieftains the helmet rising high in battle, the ringed corslet, the mighty spear. It was their custom that often both at home and in the field they should be ready for war, and equally in both positions at all such times as distress came upon their lord. Those people were good.

XX

THEY SANK THEN to sleep. One sorely paid for his evening rest, as had full often come to pass for them, when Grendel held the gold-hall, and did wickedness until the end came, death after sins. That was seen, widely known among men, that an avenger, Grendel's mother, a she-monster, yet survived the hateful one, a long while after the misery of war. She who was doomed to dwell in the dread water, the cold streams, after Cain killed his only brother, his father's son, forgot not her misery. He departed then fated, marked with murder, to flee from the joys of men; he dwelt in the wilderness. Thence sprang many fated spirits; Grendel was one of them, a hateful fierce monster; he found at Heorot a man keeping watch, waiting for war. There the monster came to grips with him; yet he remembered the power of his strength, the precious gift which God gave him, and he trusted for support, for succour and help, to Him who rules over all. By that he overcame the fiend, laid low the spirit of hell. Then he departed, the foe of mankind, in misery, reft of joy, to seek his death-dwelling. And his mother then still purposed to go on the sorrowful journey, greedy and darkly-minded, to avenge her son's death.

She came then to Heorot where the Ring-Danes slept throughout that hall. Then straightway the old fear fell on the earls, when Grendel's mother forced her way in. The dread was less by just so much as the strength of women, the war-terror of a woman, is less than a man, when the bound sword shaped by the hammer, the blood-stained blade strong in its edges, cuts off the boar-image on the foeman's helmet. Then in the hall was the strong blade drawn, the sword over the seats; many a broad buckler raised firmly in hand. He thought not of helmet nor of broad corslet, when the terror seized him.

She was in haste, was minded to go thence and save her life when she was discovered. Quickly she had seized one of the chieftains with firm grip; then she went to the fen. That was the dearest of heroes to Hrothgar among his followers between the seas, a mighty shield-warrior, whom she slew on his couch, a noble man of great fame. Beowulf was not there, but another lodging had been set apart for him earlier, after the giving of treasure to the famous Geat. There was clamour in Heorot. She had carried off the famous blood-stained hand. Care was created anew, brought to pass in the dwellings. That was no good bargain which they had to pay for in double measure with lives of friends. Then the wise king, the grey battle-warrior, was troubled in heart, when he knew that the noble thane was lifeless, that the dearest one was dead.

Beowulf was quickly brought to the castle, the victorious warrior. At dawn that earl, the noble hero himself

with his comrades, went to where the wise man was wait-
ing to see whether the All-Ruler would ever bring to pass
a change after the time of woe. Then the man famous in
fight went with his nearest followers along the floor—
(the hall-wood resounded)—till he greeted the wise one
with words, the prince of the friends of Ing; he asked if,
as he hoped, he had had a peaceful night.

XXI

Hrothgar spoke, protector of the Scyldings: "Ask thou not after happiness. Sorrow is made anew for the Danish people. Æschere is dead, Yrmenlaf's elder brother, my counsellor and my adviser, trusted friend, in such times as we fended our heads in war, when the foot-warriors crashed together and hewed the helms. Such should an earl be, a trusty chieftain, as Æschere was.

"That unjust slaughterous spirit slew him with her hands in Heorot. I know not whither the monster, made known by her feasting, journeyed back exulting in the corpse. She avenged the fight in which last night thou didst violently kill Grendel with hard grips because too long he lessened and slew my people. He fell in combat, guilty of murder, and now another mighty evil foe has come; she was minded to make requital for her son, and she has overmuch avenged the hostile deed, as it may seem to many a thane who grieves in mind for the giver of treasure with heavy heart-sorrow. Now low lies the hand which was ready for all your desires.

"I heard dwellers in the land, my people, counsellors in hall, say that they saw two such great march-steppers, alien spirits, hold the moors. One of them was, as far as they could certainly know, the likeness of a woman; the other wretched creature trod the paths of exile in man's shape, except that he was greater than any other man. Him in days past the dwellers in the land named Grendel; his father they know not; nor whether there were born to him earlier any dark spirits.

"They possess unknown land, wolf-cliffs, windy crags, a dangerous fen-path, where the mountain stream falls down under the darkness of the rocks, a flood under the earth. That is not a mile hence where the mere stands; over it hang rime-covered groves; the wood firm-rooted overshadows the water. There each night a baleful wonder may be seen, a fire on the flood. There is none so wise of the children of men who knows those depths. Though the heath-stepper hard pressed by the hounds, the hart strong in antlers, should seek the forest after a long chase, rather does he yield up his life, his spirit on the shore, than hide his head there. That is an eerie place. Thence the surge of waves mounts up dark to the clouds, when the wind stirs up hostile storms till the air darkens, the skies weep.

"Now once more help must come from thee alone. Thou dost not yet know the lair, the dangerous place, where thou mayest find the sinful creature; seek if thou darest. If thou comest away alive, I will reward thee for that onslaught, as erstwhile I did, with treasures, old precious things, twisted gold."

XXII

B EOWULF SPOKE, son of Ecgtheow: "Sorrow not, wise
warrior. It is better for each to avenge his friend than
greatly to mourn. Each of us must needs await the end of
life in the world; let him who can achieve fame ere
death. That is best for a noble warrior when life is over.
Rise up, guardian of the realm; let us go quickly hence to
behold the track of Grendel's kinswoman. I promise thee
she shall not escape under covering darkness, nor in the
earth's embrace, nor in the mountain forest, nor in the
water's depths—go where she will. Have thou, as I ex-
pect from thee, patience for all thy woes this day."

The aged one leaped up then; thanked God, the
mighty Lord, for what the man spoke. Then Hrothgar's
horse was bitted, the steed with twisted mane. The wise
prince went forth in splendour; the foot-troop of shield-
bearing warriors stepped forward. The tracks were widely
seen along the forest paths, the course over the fields.
Away over the dark moor she went; she bore the best of
thanes, reft of life, who with Hrothgar ruled the land.

Then the son of princes[1] strode over the high rocky cliffs, the narrow paths, the straitened tracks, the unknown road, the steep crags, many a monster's abode. He with a few other wise men went ahead to spy out the land, until suddenly he found the mountain trees hanging above the grey rock. The water beneath lay blood-stained and troubled. All the Danes, the friends of the Scyldings, were mournful in mood; many a thane had to suffer; there was sorrow for many of the earls, when they found Æschere's head on the cliff by the mere.

The flood surged with blood, with hot gore; the people beheld it. At times the horn sang its eager war-song. The troop all sat down; then they saw along the water many of the dragon kind, strange sea-dragons moving over the mere, also monsters lying on the rocky headlands; then at midday the dragons and wild beasts often go on a sorrowful journey on the sail-road. They fell away bitter and angered; they heard the clang, the war-horn sounding. The prince of the Geats with his bow parted one of them from life, from the struggle of the waves, so that the stout war-shaft stood in his heart. He was the more sluggish at swimming in the water, because death carried him off. Speedily the wondrous wave-dweller was hard pressed in the waves with boar-spears of deadly barbs, beset by hostile attacks and drawn out on the headland. The men beheld the dread creature.

Beowulf clad himself in warrior's armour; he lamented not his life. The war-corslet, hand-woven, broad, cunningly adorned, must needs try the water; it knew how to guard his body so that the grip of war might not wound his heart, the malicious clutch of an angry foe his life. And the gleaming helmet, which was to mingle with the depths of the mere, to seek the welter of the waves, decked with treasure, circled with diadems, as the smith of weapons wrought it in days long past, wondrously adorned it, set it round with boar-images, guarded his head so that no sword or battle-blades could pierce it. That was not the least then of mighty helps that Hrothgar's squire lent him in his need. That hilted sword was called Hrunting; it was an excellent old treasure; the brand was iron, marked with poisonous twigs, hardened in the blood of battle. It never failed any men in war who seized it with their hands, who ventured to go on dire journeys, to the meeting-place of foes. That was not the first time that it was to accomplish a mighty deed.

In truth the son of Ecglaf mighty in strength did not remember what erstwhile he spoke[2] when drunken with wine, when he lent the weapon to a better sword-warrior. He himself durst not risk his life beneath the tossing of the waves, accomplish heroic deeds. There he forfeited fame, repute for might. Not so was it with the other when he had clad himself for war.

XXIII

BEOWULF SPOKE, son of Ecgtheow: "Consider now, famous son of Healfdene, wise prince, gold-friend of warriors, now I am ready for the venture, what we spoke of a while since; if I should depart from life in thy cause, that thou shouldst ever be in the place of a father when I am gone. Be thou a guardian to my followers, my comrades, if war takes me. Likewise, dear Hrothgar, do thou send the treasures thou hast given me to Hygelac. The lord of the Geats may perceive by that gold, the son of Hrethel may see when he looks upon that treasure, that I found an excellent good giver of rings, that I took joy while I could. And do thou let Unferth have the ancient blade, the far-famed man have the precious sword with wavy pattern and sharp edge; I shall achieve fame for myself with Hrunting, or death will carry me off."

After those words the prince of the Weder-Geats hastened exceedingly; he would in no wise wait for an answer. The surge of waters received the war-hero. Then there was a spell of time ere he might behold the bottom of the mere.

She who had held for fifty years the domain of the floods, eager for battle, grim and greedy, discovered straightway that a man was seeking from above the dwelling of monsters. She reached out against him then, seized the warrior with dread claws; nevertheless she injured not the sound body; the ring-mail guarded it round about so that she could not pierce the corslet, the locked mail-shirt, with hostile fingers. When she came to the bottom, the sea-wolf bore the prince of rings to her lair, so that he could not (yet was he brave) use weapons; and too many monsters set upon him in the water, many a sea-beast rent his war-corslet with battle-tusks; they pursued the hero. Then the earl noticed he was in some kind of hostile hall, where no water in any way touched him, nor could the sudden clutch of the flood come near him because of the roofed hall; he saw the light of fire, a gleaming radiance shining brightly.

Then the valiant one perceived the she-wolf of the depths, the mighty mere-woman; he repaid the mighty rush with the battle-sword; the hand drew not back from the stroke, so that the sword, adorned with rings, sang a greedy war-chant on her head. Then the stranger found that the sword would not bite or injure life, but the edge failed the prince in his need. It had endured in times past many battles, often had cut through the helmet, the mail of a doomed man. That was the first time for the costly treasure that its repute failed.

Once again the kinsman of Hygelac was resolute, mindful of heroic deeds, no whit lax in courage. Then the angry warrior cast down the sword with its twisted ornaments, set round with decorations, so that it lay on the ground, strong and steel-edged. He trusted in his strength, his mighty hand-grip. Thus a man must needs do when he is minded to gain lasting praise in war, nor cares for his life.

Then the prince of the War-Geats seized Grendel's mother by the hair; he feared not the fight. Then stern in strife he swung the monster in his wrath so that she bent to the ground. She quickly gave him requital again with savage grips, and grasped out towards him. Weary in mood then she overthrew the strongest of fighters, the foot-warrior, so that he fell down. Then she sat on the visitor to her hall, and drew her knife, broad and bright-edged; she was minded to avenge her child, her only son. The woven breast-net lay on his shoulder; that guarded his life; it opposed the entrance of point and edge. Then the son of Ecgtheow, the hero of the Geats, would have found death under the wide waters if the war-corslet, the stout battle-net, had not afforded him help, and if holy God, the wise Lord, had not achieved victory in war; the Ruler of the heavens brought about a right issue, when once more he stood up with ease.

XXIV

HE SAW THEN among weapons a victorious blade, an old sword of giants, strong in its edges, the glory of warriors. That was the choicest of weapons; save only it was greater than any other man could bear to the battle-play, trusty and splendid, the work of giants. The hero of the Scyldings, angered and grim in battle, seized the belted hilt, wheeled the ring-marked sword, despairing of life; he struck furiously, so that it gripped her hard against the neck. It broke the bone-rings; the blade went straight through the doomed body. She fell on the floor. The brand was bloody; the man rejoiced in his work.

The gleam was bright, the light stood within, just as the candle of the sky shines serenely from heaven. He went along the dwelling; then he turned to the wall; Hygelac's thane, raging and resolute, raised the weapon firmly by its hilts. The sword was not useless to the warrior, but he was minded quickly to requite Grendel for the many onslaughts which far more than once he made on the West-Danes, when he slew Hrothgar's hearth-

companions in their sleep, devoured fifteen men of the
Danish people while they slumbered, and bore away as
many more, a hateful sacrifice. He, the furious hero,
avenged that upon him there where he saw Grendel
lying, weary of war, reft of life, as erstwhile the battle at
Heorot despatched him. The body gaped wide,[1] when
after death it suffered a stroke, a hard battle-blow: and
then he hewed off its head.

Straightway the wise men who gazed on the mere
with Hrothgar saw that the surge of waves was all trou-
bled, the water stained with blood. Grey-haired old men
spoke together of the valiant man, that they did not ex-
pect to see the chieftain again, or that he should come as
a conqueror to seek the famous prince. Then it seemed
to many that the sea-wolf had slain him. Then came the
ninth hour of the day. The bold Scyldings forsook the
headland; thence the gold-friend of men departed
homewards. The strangers sat sick at heart, and stared at
the mere; they felt desire and despair of seeing their
friendly lord himself.

Then that sword, the battle-brand, began to vanish in
drops of gore after the blood shed in fight. That was a
great wonder, that it all melted like ice when the Father
loosens the bond of the frost, unbinds the fetters of the
floods; He has power over times and seasons. That is the
true Lord.

The prince of the Weder-Geats took no more of the
precious hoardings in those haunts, though he saw many
there, save the head and with it the treasure-decked
hilts. The sword had melted before, the inlaid brand had
burned away, so hot was that blood and so poisonous the
alien spirit who died in it. Straightway he fell to swim-
ming; he, who before in the struggle endured the fall of

foes, dived up through the water. The wave-surges were all cleansed, the great haunts where the alien spirit gave up his life and this fleeting state.

Then the protector of sea-men, brave-minded, came swimming to land; he took pleasure in the sea-booty, in the mighty burden which he bore with him. They went to meet him, the excellent troop of thanes; they thanked God; they rejoiced in the prince, that they could behold him safe and sound. Then helm and corslet were loosed with speed from off the brave man; the lake lay still, the water under the clouds, stained with the blood of battle.

They set out thence on the foot-tracks, joyous at heart; they paced the path, the well-known street. Men nobly bold bore the head from the cliff with toil for each of the very brave ones. Four men with difficulty had to carry Grendel's head to the gold-hall on the battle-spear, until of a sudden the fourteen brave warlike Geats came to the hall; their lord trod the fields about the mead-hall with them, fearless among his followers.

Then the prince of thanes, the man bold in deeds, made glorious with fame, the hero terrible in battle, came in to greet Hrothgar. Then Grendel's head was borne by the hair into the hall where the men were drinking—a dread object for the earls and the queen with them; the men looked at the wondrous sight.

XXV

B EOWULF SPOKE, son of Ecgtheow: "Lo! son of Healf-
dene, prince of the Scyldings, we have brought thee
with pleasure, as a token of glory, these sea-trophies
which thou beholdest here. Scarcely did I survive that
with my life, the struggle beneath the water, barely did I
accomplish the task, the fight was all but ended, if God
had not protected me.

"I could do naught with Hrunting in the fight, though
that weapon is worthy, but the Ruler of men vouchsafed
that I should see a huge old sword hang gleaming on
the wall—most often He has guided those bereft of
friends—so that I swung the weapon. Then in the strug-
gle I slew the guardians of the house when the chance
was given me. Then that battle-brand, the inlaid sword,
burned away as soon as the blood spurted out, hottest
battle-gore. Thence from the foes I carried off that hilt; I
avenged, as was fitting, the deeds of malice, the massacre
of the Danes.

"So I promise thee that thou mayest sleep in Heorot,

free from sorrow with the band of thy warriors and all the thanes among thy people, the youths and veterans; that thou, prince of the Scyldings, dost not need to dread death for the earls from the quarter thou didst formerly."

Then the gold hilt, the ancient work of giants, was given into the hands of the old warrior, the grey-haired leader. It came into the possession of the prince of the Danes, the work of cunning smiths, after the death of the monsters, and after the creature of hostile heart, God's foe, guilty of murder, and his mother also had left this world. It came into the power of the best of mighty kings between the seas who dealt out money in Scandinavia.

Hrothgar spoke; he beheld the hilt, the old heirloom. On it was written the beginning of a battle of long ago, when a flood, a rushing sea, slew the race of giants; they had lived boldly; that race was estranged from the eternal Lord. The Ruler gave them final requital for that in the surge of the water. Thus on the plates of bright gold it was clearly marked, set down and expressed in runic letters, for whom that sword, the best of blades, was first wrought with its twisted haft and snake images.

Then the wise man spoke, the son of Healfdene. All were silent. "Lo! he who achieves truth and right among the people may say that this earl was born excellent (the old ruler of the realm recalls all things from the past). Thy renown is raised up throughout the wide ways, my friend Beowulf, among all peoples. Thou preservest all steadfastly, thy might with wisdom of mind. I shall show thee my favour, as before we agreed. Thou shalt be granted for long years as a solace to thy people, as a help to heroes.

"Not so did Heremod[1] prove to the sons of Ecgwela, the honourable Scyldings; his way was not as they wished, but to the slaughter and butchery of the people of the Danes. Savage in mood he killed his table-companions, his trusty counsellors, until he, the famous prince, departed alone from the joys of men, although mighty God had made him great by the joys of power and by strength, had raised him above all men. Yet there grew in his heart a bloodthirsty brood of thoughts. He gave out no rings to the Danes according to custom; joyless he dwelt, so that he reaped the reward of his hostility, the long evil to his people. Learn thou by this; lay hold on virtue. I have spoken this for thy good from the wisdom of many years.

"It is wonderful to tell how mighty God with his generous thought bestows on mankind wisdom, land and rank. He has dominion over all things. At times He allows man's thoughts to turn to love of famous lineage; He gives him in his land the joys of domain, the stronghold of men to keep. He puts the parts of the world, a wide kingdom, in such subjection to him that he cannot in his folly conceive an end to that. He lives in plenty; nothing afflicts him, neither sickness nor age; nor does sorrow darken his mind, nor does strife anywhere show forth sword-hatred, but all the world meets his desire.

XXVI

"HE KNOWS NOTHING worse till within him his pride grows and springs up. Then the guardian slumbers, the keeper of the soul—the sleep is too heavy—pressed round with troubles; the murderer very near who shoots maliciously from his bow. Then he is stricken in the breast under the helmet by a sharp shaft—he knows not how to guard himself—by the crafty evil commands of the ill spirit. That which he had long held seems to him too paltry, he covets fiercely, he bestows no golden rings in generous pride, and he forgets and neglects the destiny which God, the Ruler of glory, formerly gave him, his share of honours. At the end it comes to pass that the mortal body sinks into ruin, falls doomed; another comes to power who bestows treasures gladly, old wealth of the earl; he takes joy in it. Keep thyself from such passions, dear Beowulf, best of warriors, and choose for thyself that better part, lasting profit. Care not for pride, famous hero. Now the repute of thy might endures for a space; straightway again shall age, or edge of the sword, part thee from thy strength, or the embrace of fire, or the surge of the flood, or the grip of the blade, or the flight of the spear, or hateful old age, or the gleam of eyes shall pass away and be darkened; on a sudden it shall come to pass that death shall vanquish thee, noble warrior.

"Thus have I ruled over the Ring-Danes under the heavens for fifty years, and guarded them by my war-power from many tribes throughout this world, from spears and swords, so that I thought I had no foe under the stretch of the sky. Lo! a reverse came upon me in my land, sorrow after joy, when Grendel grew to be a foe of many years, my visitant. I suffered great sorrow of heart continually from that persecution. Thanks be to God, the eternal Lord, that I have survived with my life, that I behold with my eyes that blood-stained head after the old struggle. Go now to the seat, enjoy the banquet, thou who art made illustrious by war; very many treasures shall be parted between us when morning comes."

The Geat was glad in mind; straightway he went to seek out his seat as the wise man bade him. Then again as before the meal was fairly spread once more for men in hall famed for their courage. The covering night grew dark over the noble warriors. The veterans all rose up; the grey-haired aged Scylding was minded to seek his bed. It pleased the Geat, the mighty shield-warrior, exceeding well to rest. Forthwith a hall-thane, who ministered in fitting fashion to all the needs of a thane which the warlike seafarers should have that day, guided him forth, weary as he was from his journey, come from afar. The great-hearted man took his rest; the building towered up wide-gabled and gold-plated; the guest slumbered within till the black raven merrily proclaimed the joy of heaven.

Then came the bright light gliding after the shadow. The warriors hastened, the chieftains were ready to go again to their people, the stout-hearted sojourner was minded to seek the boat far thence. Then the brave man, the son of Ecglaf, bade him bear Hrunting, take his sword, his dear blade; he thanked him for the gift; said that he counted him a good friend in battle, mighty in war; in no wise did he belittle the sword's edge; that was a brave warrior. And the men of war then, ready in war-trappings, were about to depart; the chieftain, dear to the Danes, went to the throne where the other was, the hero dreaded in battle; he greeted Hrothgar.

XXVII

BEOWULF SPOKE, son of Ecgtheow: "Now we seafarers, come from afar, wish to say that we purpose to seek Hygelac. We have been as kindly treated here as we could wish; thou hast been good unto us. If I can in any way on earth win a greater love from thee, lord of men, for warlike deeds than I have yet done, I am ready forthwith. If beyond the compass of the floods I hear that thy neighbours press upon thee with dread war, as at times foes have done to thee, I shall bring to thy help a thousand thanes and heroes. I know that Hygelac, the lord of the Geats, protector of the people, though he is young, will aid me in words and deeds to support thee well and bear a spear to thy aid, mighty succour, if thou hast need of men. If Hrethric, a prince's son, betake himself to the court of the Geats, he may find many friends there. For him who trusts his own merit it is better to visit distant lands."

Hrothgar spoke to him in answer: "The wise Lord has sent those speeches into thy mind. I have not heard a man of such young age discourse more wisely. Thou art strong in might and wise in mind, prudent in speeches. It is my expectation, if it comes to pass that the spear, grim war, sickness, or steel should carry off the son of Hrethel, thy prince, the protector of the people, and thou art still alive, that the Sea-Geats will have no better king to choose, treasure-guardian of heroes, if thou wilt rule the kingdom of thy kinsmen. Thy mind pleases me the better as time goes on, dear Beowulf. Thou hast brought it to pass that there shall be peace between the peoples, the men of the Geats and the Spear-Danes, and that strife shall cease, the treacherous hostility they formerly suffered; while I rule over the wide realm treasures shall be in common; many a man shall greet another with gifts across the gannet's bath; the ring-prowed ship shall bear offerings and love-tokens over the sea. I know the people from old tradition to be wholly blameless towards friend and foe when they are of one mind."

Then moreover the protector of earls, the son of Healfdene, gave in the house twelve treasures; he bade him seek his dear people in safety with those offerings, come again speedily. Then the king of noble race, the prince of the Scyldings, kissed the best of thanes, and fell upon his neck; tears fell from him, the grey-haired man. There was the chance of two things for him, the old man full of years, but more of one, that they should not see one another again, brave men in talk together. That man was so dear to him, that he could not stifle the trouble in his heart, but, fast bound in the thoughts of his heart, the secret longing for the loved man burned in his blood. Thence Beowulf strode over the grass meadow, the warrior proud of his gold, glorying in treasure. The sea-goer riding at anchor awaited its lord. Then Hrothgar's gift was often praised on the voyage. That was a king blameless in all ways, till old age, which has done hurt to many, robbed him of the joys of strength.

XXVIII

THEN THE TROOP of exceeding brave warriors came to the flood; they bore ring-woven corslets, locked shirts of mail. The watchman spied the return of the earls as erstwhile he did.

He did not salute the strangers from the edge of the cliff with insult, but rode towards them; he told the people of the Weders that the warriors with gleaming armour went welcome to the ship. Then the spacious ship laden with war garments was on the sand, the ring-prowed vessel with horses and treasures; the mast towered aloft above Hrothgar's precious hoardings.

He gave to the guardian of the ship a sword bound with gold, so that afterwards on the mead-bench he was the more esteemed for the treasure, the ancient sword. He embarked on the ship, to plough the deep water; left the land of the Danes. Then by the mast was a sea-cloth, a sail bound by a rope. The timbers creaked; the wind over the billows did not force the wave-floater from her course. The sea-goer went on her way, the foamy-necked

one floated forth over the waves, the boat with bound
prow over the ocean-streams, till they could see the cliffs
of the Geats, the well-known headlands. The boat drove
ashore; urged by the wind it rested on the land.

Quickly the haven-watchman, who for a long time had
gazed out afar at the waters expecting the dear men, was
ready by the sea. He bound the broad-bosomed ship to
the sand firmly with anchor-bonds, lest the might of the
waves should drive away the winsome vessel. Then he[1]
bade the treasure of chieftains, adornments and beaten
gold, to be carried up. He had not far to go thence to
seek the giver of treasure, Hygelac, son of Hrethel,
where he dwells at home, himself with his comrades
near the sea-wall.

The house was splendid, the ruler a mighty king in
the high hall, Hygd[2] very young, wise, high-minded, al-
though she, the daughter of Hæreth, had lived few years
in the stronghold. Yet was she not petty, nor too grudging
in gifts and treasures to the people of the Geats. She, the
splendid queen of the people, had not the pride or the
dread hostility of Thryth.[3] No brave one of the dear com-
rades, except the mighty prince, durst venture to look
upon her openly with his eyes; but he might count upon
deadly bonds hand-woven made ready for him. Quickly
after that the wrong-doer was destined to the sword, so
that the inlaid brand might give judgment, might pro-
claim the deadly evil. Such is not queenly usage for a
woman to practise, though she is splendid; that she who
was meant to establish peace[4] should seek the life of a
dear subject because of fancied wrong. In truth the kins-
men of Hemming detested that.

Men at their ale-drinking told another tale, that she
brought less evils on the people, crafty acts of malice, as

soon as she was given, gold-adorned, to the young warrior, to the brave chieftain, when by her father's counsel she sought in her journey the hall of Offa over the yellow flood, where afterwards on the throne she well employed while she lived what was granted her in life, a good famous woman.[5] She kept a noble love towards the prince of heroes, the best, as I have heard, of all mankind, of the race of men between the seas. For Offa was a skilled spearman, widely honoured for gifts and victories; he ruled his realm with wisdom. From him sprang Eomær for a help to heroes, kinsman of Hemming, grandson of Garmund, mighty in onslaught.[6]

XXIX

THEN THE BOLD man went himself with his troop to tread the meadow by the sea, the wide shores. The world-candle shone, the sun bright from the south. They went on their way; quickly they marched till they heard that the protector of earls, the slayer of Ongentheow,[1] the worthy young war-king, was bestowing rings in the court. Beowulf's arrival was quickly proclaimed to Hygelac, that the defender of warriors, the shield-comrade, was come alive to the palace there, to the court, unscathed from the battle-play.

With speed, as the mighty one ordered, a space was cleared within the hall for the new-comers. Then he who survived the combat sat down opposite him, kinsman opposite kinsman, when in solemn speech with chosen words he greeted his gracious lord. The daughter of Hæreth went about throughout that hall-building with mead-vessels; she loved the people, bore the flagon to the hands of the Heath-dwellers. Hygelac began graciously to question his companion in the high hall; desire to know the exploits of the Sea-Geats was strong upon him.

"How fared ye on the voyage, dear Beowulf, when on a sudden thou hadst desire to seek combat afar over the salt water, warfare at Heorot? Surely thou hast somewhat mended for Hrothgar, the famous prince, his wide-known sorrow? In my heart's grief for that I was troubled with surgings of sorrow; I put no trust in my loved man's venture; long while I besought thee that thou shouldst have naught to do with the murderous monster, let the South-Danes themselves fight out the struggle with Grendel. I utter thanks to God, that it is granted me to behold thee unscathed."

Beowulf spoke, son of Ecgtheow: "That is known, my lord Hygelac, to many men, the famous encounter; what struggle there was between Grendel and me in that place, where he brought very many sorrows upon the victorious Scyldings, lasting oppression. I avenged all that. Thus none of Grendel's kin upon earth has cause to boast of that uproar at dawn, not he who lives longest of the loathly race, snared in sin.

"Even there did I come to that ring-hall to greet Hrothgar. Straightway the famous son of Healfdene, when he knew my purpose, assigned me a seat beside his own son. His troop was making merry; I have never seen under the vault of heaven greater mead-joy of men sitting in hall. At times the famous queen, she who establishes peace among the peoples, moved throughout the hall, encouraged the young men; often she gave a ring to a warrior ere she went to her seat. At times Hrothgar's daughter bore the ale-flagon before the veterans, to the earls in the high places; then I heard men sitting in hall name Freawaru, where she bestowed the nail-studded

vessel on the heroes; she, young, gold-adorned, is prom-
ised to the gracious son of Froda.[2] The friend of the
Scyldings, the ruler of the realm, has brought that about,
and counts it a gain that he should settle with the woman
a part of his deadly feuds and struggles.[3] It is always a
rare thing, when a little while after the fall of the prince
the murderous spear sinks to rest, even though the bride
is of worth.

XXX

"THAT MAY RANKLE with the prince of the Heatho-
bards and each thane among the people, when he
goes in hall with the bride, that a noble scion of the
Danes should tend the warriors. On him gleams the ar-
mour[1] of his forefathers, hard and ringmarked, the trea-
sure of the Heathobards, whilst they were able to wield
those weapons, until they led their dear comrades and
themselves to ruin at the shield-play.

"Then an old spear-warrior who gazes on the treasure,
who bears in mind all the slaughter of men, speaks at the
beer-drinking—grim is his heart—he begins in mournful
mood to test the thoughts of the young warrior by the
musings of his mind, to stir up evil strife—and he utters
these words:

" 'Canst thou, my friend, recognise the sword, the
precious blade, thy father bore to battle, where the
Danes slew him when under his helmet for the last time;
the bold Scyldings held the field when Withergyld lay
low, after the fall of heroes. Now some youth or other of

78

those murderers exulting in his adornments walks here
in the hall; boasts of the slaughter and wears the trea-
sure, which thou shouldst rightfully own.'

"Thus at all times he admonishes and stirs up memo-
ries with baneful words till the season comes when the
bride's thane[2] slumbers, stained with blood after the
sword-stroke, his life forfeited because of her father's
deeds. The other escapes with his life, he knows the
country well. Then on both sides are broken the solemn
oaths of earls. Afterwards deadly hatreds surge up
against Ingeld, and his love for his wife grows cooler
from his anguish of mind. Wherefore I look not for the
good-will of the Heathobards, nor for much loyalty, void
of malice, to the Danes, nor firm friendship.

"I shall speak on once again about Grendel, that thou,
the giver of treasure, mayest know well what was later
the issue of the hand-struggle of heroes.

"After the jewel of the sky glided over the fields, the
monster came raging, the dread night-foe, to seek us out,
where safe and sound we held the hall. There was war
fatal to Hondscio, a violent death to the doomed man.
He was the first to fall, the girded warrior. Grendel de-
voured him, the famous liege-man; he swallowed the
whole body of the loved man. Nevertheless the bloody
toothed slayer, his thought set on evil, was not minded to
go out again from the gold-hall empty-handed; but,
strong in his might, he pitted himself against me, laid
hold with ready hand. A pouch[3] hung wide and won-
drous, made firm with artful clasps; it was all cunningly
devised by the power of the devil and with dragon skins.
He, the savage worker of deeds, purposed to put me into
it, though guiltless, with many others; it could not come
to pass thus when I stood upright in my wrath.

"It is too long to tell how I gave requital to the people's foe for every ill deed. There, my prince, did I bring honour on thy people by my deeds. He escaped forth; for a short space he enjoyed the pleasures of life; yet his right hand remained in Heorot for a token of him; and he, departing thence wretched, sank down, sad in mind, to the bottom of the mere.

"When morning came and we had sat down to the banquet, the friend of the Scyldings rewarded me richly for the deadly onslaught with beaten gold, with many treasures. There was singing and merriment. An aged Scylding of great experience told tales of long ago. At times one bold in battle drew sweetness from the harp, the joy-wood; at times wrought a measure true and sad; at times the large-hearted king told a wondrous story in fitting fashion. At times again an old warrior bowed down with age began to speak to the youths of prowess in fight; his heart swelled within him, when, old in years, he brought to mind many things.

"Thus we took our pleasure there the livelong day, till another night came to men. Then forthwith again Grendel's mother was ready to avenge her grief; sorrowful, she journeyed. Death, the hostility of the Weders, had carried off her son. The monstrous woman avenged her child, she slew a warrior in her might. There life went out from Æschere, a wise councillor through many years. Nor, when morning came, might they, the men of the Danes, consume with fire him who had been made powerless by death; nor lay the loved man on the pyre. She bore off that body in a fiend's embrace under the mountain stream. That was to Hrothgar the heaviest of the sorrows which for a long while had laid hold on the prince of the people. Then the prince, lamenting, entreated me

by thy life, that, in the press of the floods, I should per-
form a deed of prowess, should hazard my life, should
achieve an heroic exploit. He promised me reward. Then
I found the grim, terrible guardian of the depths of the
surging water, who is known far and wide. There for a
space was hand-to-hand grappling; the water welled with
blood, and in that hall in the depths I cut off the head of
Grendel's mother with a gigantic sword; with violence I
tore her life from her; I was not yet doomed to death,
but the protector of earls, the son of Healfdene, gave me
again many a treasure.

XXXI

"THUS DID THE king of the people live as was fitting; in no way did I lose the rewards, the guerdon of my strength; but he, the son of Healfdene, gave me treasures into my own keeping. Them I will bring and gladly proffer to thee, king of warriors. Once more all favours come from thee. I have few close kinsmen save thee, Hygelac."

Then he commanded to be brought in the boar-image, the banner, the helmet riding high in battle, the grey corslet, the splendid war-sword. Afterwards he spoke:

"Hrothgar, the wise prince, gave me this battle-garment; he expressly bade that I should first declare his good-will to thee. He said that king Heorogar,[1] prince of the Scyldings, had it, the breast-armour, for a long space; that nevertheless he would not give it to his son, the bold Heoroweard, though he was loyal to him. Use all things well."

I heard that four horses, reddish yellow, every whit

alike, came next in order; he gave him possession of steeds and stores; thus must a kinsman do, and not weave a cunning net for another, prepare death for a comrade with secret guile. To Hygelac, stout in fight, his nephew was very loyal, and each was mindful of the other's pleasure.

I heard that he presented to Hygd that neck-band, the precious, wondrous treasure, which Wealtheow, the prince's daughter, gave him, together with three steeds full of grace and furnished with gleaming saddles. When she had taken the ring her breast was made fair.

Thus the son of Ecgtheow, a man famous in battle, was bold in brave deeds; he lived honourably; never did he slay his hearth-companions in his drunkenness; his was not a savage mind, but, fearless in fight, he guarded the precious gift which God had given him with the greatest strength among men. Long was he despised,[2] for the men of the Geats accounted him worthless; nor was the lord of troops minded to do him much honour on the mead-bench; they thought indeed that he was slothful, an unfit chieftain. A recompense came to the famous man for every slight.

Then the protector of earls, the king mighty in battle, bade them bring in the sword of Hrethel,[3] decked with gold; there was not at that time with the Geats a better treasure among swords; he laid that in Beowulf's bosom, and gave him seven thousand measures of land, a house and princely rank. To them both in that country land, domain, ancestral claims, had come by natural right, but more to Hygelac, a wide realm, in that he was the more illustrious.

It came to pass in later days among the warriors, when Hygelac was laid low and battle-swords slew Heardred[4] under cover of his shield, after the bold battle-heroes, the warlike Scylfings, sought him mid his victorious troop, pressed hard in fight the nephew of Hereric, that then the wide realm came under Beowulf's sway. He ruled well for fifty years—he was then an aged king, an old guardian of the land—till a dragon which guarded treasure in a burial mound, a steep rock, began to show his might on the dark nights. A pathway lay beneath, unknown to men; some man entered there, greedily seized the pagan hoard . . . tricked the keeper of the treasure with thievish cunning while he slept . . . so that he was enraged.[5]

XXXII

HE WHO DID himself sore hurt did not violate the dragon's hoard eagerly of his own free will; but some thane of the sons of heroes was fleeing in great distress from hostile blows, and pressed down by his guilt, lacking a shelter, the man took hiding there. Straightway he looked in . . . dread of the monster lay upon him, yet in his misery . . . then the sudden attack seized him. . . .[1]

There were in the cave many such ancient treasures, which in days gone by some men carefully hid there, great relics of a noble race, precious store.

Death took them all off in past times, and still that one veteran of the people who tarried there longest, a watchman wearying for his friends, looked toward the like fate, that but for a short space he might have sway over the long-gathered treasures. The barrow stood all ready on open ground, hard by the waves, newly-raised near the headland, strong in artful barriers. Into it the guardian of the rings bore the precious heap of the treasures of earls, of beaten gold. Few words he spoke:

"Now, earth, do thou hold, now that heroes cannot, the wealth of earls! Lo! valiant men erstwhile took it from thee. Death in war, a sweeping slaughter, took off each of the men, each of my people, who gave up this life; they had seen joy in hall. I have no one who can wield the sword or polish the golden vessel, the precious flagon; the old warriors have departed. The stout helmet adorned with gold must be reft of its beaten plates. The polishers slumber who should make splendid the battle-masks; and the corslet likewise, which endured the stroke of swords in war mid the cracking of shields, follows the warrior to decay. The coat of mail cannot journey afar by the side of heroes after the passing of the warrior. There is no joy of the harp, delight of the timbrel, nor does the good hawk sweep through the hall, nor the swift steed stamp in the court. Violent death has caused to pass many generations of men."

Thus, sad in mind, the latest left of all lamented his sorrow; day and night he wept joyless, till the surge of death touched his heart. The old twilight-foe, the naked hostile dragon, who seeks out barrows, flaming as he goes, who flies by night compassed with fire, found the costly treasure. Him the dwellers in the land greatly fear. He must needs seek the hoard in the earth, where, old in years, he holds possession of the pagan gold; nor shall he profit one whit by that.

Thus did the people's foe guard that mighty treasure-house in the earth for three hundred years, till a man angered him in mind. He bore the plated goblet to his master, begged his lord for protection. Then the treasure was found, the hoard of rings was lessened; the boon was granted to the unhappy man. For the first time the prince beheld the ancient work of men.

Then the dragon awoke, wrath was rekindled; he sprang along the rock; brave in heart, he came upon the enemy's foot-track; he had stepped with stealthy craft near the dragon's head. Thus may a man, not destined to fall, who relies on the Almighty's protection, easily survive sorrow and exile.

The treasure-guardian, sore and savage in mind, made eager search along the ground; was set on finding the man, him who had done him scathe while he slept; often he made a whole circuit of the mound outside. There was no man in that waste place. Yet he was keen for the conflict, the work of war; at times he turned to the barrow, sought the treasure. Forthwith he found that some man had ransacked the gold, the rich stores. With difficulty did the treasure-guardian delay till evening came; then wrathful was the warden of the barrow; the foul creature was determined to avenge with fire the precious flagon.

Then day had departed, as the dragon desired; no longer would he wait on the wall, but went forth with fire, furnished with flame. The first onslaught was terrifying to the people in the land, even as it was speedily ended with sorrow for their giver of treasure.

Then the monster began to belch forth flames, to burn the bright dwellings. The flare of the fire brought fear upon men. The loathly air-flier wished not to leave aught living there. The warring of the dragon was widely seen, the onslaught of the cruel foe far and near, how the enemy of the people of the Geats wrought despite and devastation. He hastened back to the hoard, to his hidden hall, ere it was day. He had compassed the dwellers in the land with fire, with flames and with burning; he trusted in the barrow, in bravery and the rampart. His hope deceived him.

XXXIII

THEN QUICKLY THE terror was made known to Beowulf according to the truth, that his own abode, the best of buildings, the gift-throne of the Geats, was melting in the surges of flame. That was sorrow to the good man's soul, greatest of griefs to the heart. The wise man thought that, breaking established law, he had bitterly angered God, the Lord everlasting. His breast was troubled within by dark thoughts, as was not his wont.

The fire-dragon had destroyed with flames the stronghold of his subjects, the land by the sea from without, the countryside. The warlike king, the prince of the Weders, gave him requital for that. Then the protector of warriors, the lord of earls, bade an iron shield, a splendid war-targe, to be wrought for him. Full well he knew that wood could not help him; linden wood against fire. The chieftain long famous was fated to endure the end of fleeting days, of life in the world, and the dragon with him, though for long space he had held the treasure-store.

Then the prince of rings scorned to seek the far-flier with a troop of men, with a great host. He feared not the fight, nor did he account as aught the valour of the dragon, his power and prowess; because ere this, defying danger, he had come through many onslaughts, wild attacks, when he, the man of victory, purged Hrothgar's hall, and in war killed with his grip the kin of Grendel, the hateful race.

That was not the most paltry of hand-to-hand struggles, where they slew Hygelac, when the king of the Geats, the friendly prince of the peoples, the son of Hrethel, died in the rushes of battle in the land of the Frisians, his blood shed by the sword, beaten down by the brand. Beowulf came thence by his own strength; swam over the sea. Alone he held on his arm thirty suits of armour when he set out on the sea. The Hetware,[1] who bore the linden shields forward against him, had no cause to boast of the battle on foot. Few escaped from that battle-hero to seek their home. The son of Ecgtheow swam over the stretch of the gulfs, the hapless solitary man back to his people, where Hygd tendered him treasure and kingdom, rings and the throne; she did not trust her son, that he could hold his fatherland against hostile hosts, now that Hygelac was dead.

Yet the unhappy men could in no way win the chieftain's consent that he would be lord over Heardred, or that he would elect to rule the realm.[2] Nevertheless he upheld him among the people with friendly counsel, graciously with support, until Heardred grew older; he ruled the Weder-Geats.[3] Exiles, the sons of Ohtere,[4] sought him over the sea. They had risen against the protector of the Scylfings, the best of sea-kings who gave out treasure in Sweden, a famous prince. That ended his life. Deadly wounds from sword-slashes he, the son of Hygelac, gained there for his hospitality; and the son of Ongentheow departed again to seek his home when Heardred was laid low; he let Beowulf hold the throne, rule over the Geats. That was a good king.

XXXIV

I N AFTER DAYS he forgot not requital for the prince's fall; he became a friend to the wretched Eadgils.[1] He aided the son of Ohtere overseas with a troop, with warriors and weapons. He took vengeance afterwards with cold, sad marches; he deprived the king of life.

Thus he, the son of Ecgtheow, had survived every onslaught, dread battles, mighty ventures, until that day when he was to encounter the dragon. The lord of the Geats went then with eleven others, raging with anger, to behold the dragon. He had heard then whence the feud arose, the hostility of warriors; the famous costly vessel came into his possession through the hand of the finder.

He who brought about the beginning of that strife, fettered, sad in mind, was the thirteenth man in the troop; he was forced, though in misery, to show the way. He went against his will, till he could spy that cave, the barrow under the ground, hard by the surge of the waters, the struggle of the waves. Within, it was full of jewels and wire ornaments. The monstrous guardian, the ready fighter, grown old beneath the earth, held the treasures. That was no easy matter for any man to enter there.

The king, mighty in onslaught, sat down then on the headland, whilst he, the gold-friend of the Geats, wished good fortune to his hearth-companions. His mind was sad, restless, brooding on death; fate exceeding near which was destined to come on the old man, to seek the treasure of his soul, to part asunder life from the body. Not for long after that was the chieftain's spirit clothed in flesh.

Beowulf spoke, son of Ecgtheow: "In my youth I came through many rushes of war, times of combat. I remember all that. I was seven years old when the prince of treasures, the friendly ruler of the peoples, took me from my father; King Hrethel brought me up and fostered me, bestowed on me treasure and banqueting, bore in mind our kinship; in his life I was no less loved by him, a child in the court, than any of his children, Herebeald and Hæthcyn, or my Hygelac. For the eldest a bed of death was made ready by deeds not fit for a kinsman, when Hæthcyn smote him with curved bow, his friendly prince with an arrow; he missed his mark and shot his kinsman, one brother the other with bloody shaft. That was a violent deed not to be atoned for by gifts, cunningly wrought, weighing sore on the heart. Yet in spite of that the chieftain must needs pass from life unavenged.

"In like manner it is sad for an aged man to endure, that his son in his youth should swing from the gallows. Then he makes a measure, a song of sorrow, when his son hangs, a delight for the raven,[2] and he, aged and full of years, can in no way bring him help. He is ever reminded each morning of his son's death; he cares not to await the birth of another son in his court after the one has made acquaintance with evil deeds by the agony of death. Sorrowful he gazes on his son's room, the deserted wine-hall, a resting-place for the winds, reft of noise. The horsemen slumber, the heroes in their graves; there is no music of the harp, joy in the palace, as there was of yore.

XXXV

"He goes then to his sleeping-place, sings a song of sorrow, one man for another; his lands and dwelling seemed all too spacious for him. Thus did the protector of the Weders bear surging sorrow in his heart for Herebeald; he could no whit avenge the murderous deed on the slayer. Nor could he work hurt to the warrior, though he was not dear to him. Then with that grief which came sorely upon him, he forsook joy of men, chose God's light; left to his sons, as a worthy man does, land and cities, when he departed from life.

"Then guilt and strife came to be the portion of Swedes and Geats over the wide water, a bitter hostility after Hrethel died, and Ongentheow's sons were brave and bold in fight. They did not wish to keep up friendship over the lakes, but often they cunningly contrived dread slaughter near Hreosnaburh. That did my friendly kinsmen avenge, the feud and the outrage, as was well known, though one of them paid for it at a dear price with his life. To Hæthcyn,[1] lord of the Geats, war proved fatal. Then I heard that in the morning one brother avenged the other on the slayer with the sword-edge. There Ongentheow seeks out Eofor. The war-helmet was shattered, the aged Scylfing fell mortally stricken; the hand forgot not the feud; it drew not back from the deadly blow.

"With gleaming sword I repaid in war, as chance was given me, the treasures he[2] bestowed on me. He gave me land, domain, an ancestral seat. There was no need for him to seek among the Gepidæ,[3] or the Spear-Danes, or in the kingdom of the Swedes for less worthy warriors, to buy them with treasure. Ever I wished to be before him on foot, alone in the van, and so shall I do battle while my life lasts, while this sword endures that early and late has often followed me. Afterwards I slew Dæghrefn, the champion of the Hugas, in the presence of the veterans. He was not able at all to bring adornments, breast-ornaments, to the king of the Frisians, but the keeper of the banner, the chieftain in his might, fell amid the warriors. The sword was not the slayer, but my battle-grip crushed the surges of his heart and his body. Now the edge of the sword, the hand and the keen blade, shall wage war for the treasure."

Beowulf spoke, he uttered pledges for the last time: "In my youth I passed through many battles; yet I, aged protector of the people, wish to seek the fight, to achieve the heroic deed, if the foul foe comes out of his cave to face me."

Then for the last time he greeted each of the men, brave bearers of helmets, dear comrades: "I would not bear a sword, a weapon against the dragon, if I knew how else I could make good my boast against the monster, as erstwhile I did against Grendel; but here I expect hot battle-flame, a blast of breath, and poison. Wherefore I bear shield and corslet. I will not give back the space of a foot before the keeper of the barrow, but the fight shall be between us at the wall, as Fate, the master of every man, shall decide for us. I am brave in mind, so that I can keep from boasting against the winged fighter. Do ye, clad in corslets, warriors in battle-array, bide on the barrow to see which of us two can better survive wounds after the deadly onslaught. This is not your venture, nor is it in any man's power, except mine alone, to strive with his strength against the monster, to perform heroic deeds. With my might I shall gain the gold; or war, a perilous violent death, shall carry off your prince."

Then by his shield the strong warrior arose, stern under his helmet; he bore the battle-corslet under the rocky cliffs; he trusted in the strength of a single man. Such is no coward's venture.

Then he, excellent in virtues, who had survived very many combats, wild attacks, when foot-warriors crashed together, saw a stone arch standing by the wall, a stream gushing out thence from the barrow. The surge of the spring was hot with battle-fires; by reason of the dragon's flame he could not endure for any time unburnt the recess near the treasure. The prince of the Weder-Geats, when he was angered, let a word go out from his breast; the strong-hearted man was wrathful; his voice loud in battle went in resounding under the grey stone.

Hate was roused, the treasure-guardian heard the speech of a man; there was no longer time to seek friendship; first the monster's breath, hot sweat of battle, issued out from the stone; the earth resounded. The warrior, lord of the Geats, swung his shield under the barrow against the dread creature. Then the heart of the coiling dragon

was ready to seek strife. The valiant warlike king first bran-
dished the sword, the ancient blade, not dull in its edges.
Each of the two hostile-minded ones felt fear of the other.
The ruler of friends stood staunchly against his high
shield, when the dragon quickly coiled together; he waited
in his war-gear. Then striding amid flames, contorted he
went, hastening to his fate. The shield guarded life and
body well for the famous prince less time than he wished.
There then for the first time he had to show his strength
without Fate allotting him fame in battle. The lord of the
Geats raised up his hand, he struck the dread gleaming
monster with the precious sword, so that the bright edge
turned on the bone; it bit less keenly than its king, hard
pressed by trouble, had need. Then after the battle-stroke
the guardian of the treasure was in savage mood; he cast
forth deadly fire; far leaped the war-flames. The gold-
friend of the Geats boasted not of famous victories; the
naked battle-blade failed at need, as it should not have
done, the long-famous brand. That was no easy step for
the famous son of Ecgtheow to consent to yield that
ground; against his will he must needs inhabit a dwelling
elsewhere; thus must every man forsake fleeting days.

It was not long till the fighters closed again. The
treasure-guardian took heart anew. His breast laboured
with breathing. He who before held sway over the peo-
ple suffered anguish, ringed round with fire.

No whit did his comrades, sons of chieftains, stand
about him in a band with valour, but they took to the
wood, they hid for their lives. In one of them the mind
was roused to face sorrows. In him who well considers
nothing can ever stifle kinship.

XXXVI

HE WAS CALLED Wiglaf, son of Weohstan, a valued shield-warrior, prince of the Scylfings, kinsman of Ælfhere;[1] he saw his lord suffering the heat under his war-helm. Then he called to mind the favour which formerly he had bestowed on him, the rich dwelling-place of the Wægmundings, all the rights his father possessed. He could not then hold back; his hand seized the shield, the yellow linden wood, drew the ancient sword, that was among men a relic of Eanmund, son of Ohtere. Weohstan slew him in battle with the edge of the sword, a friendless exile, and bore off from his kin the bright gleaming helm, the ringed corslet, the gigantic old sword that Onela gave him, his kinsman's war-trappings, ready battle-equipment. He spoke not of the feud, though he[2] had killed his brother's child. Many years he held the adornments, brand and corslet until his son could achieve mighty deeds like his old father. Then when he departed from life, old in his passing hence, he gave among the Geats an exceeding number of battle-garments.

That was the first time that the young warrior was to stand the rush of battle with his prince. His spirit did not weaken, nor did his father's sword fail in the fight. The dragon discovered that when they had come together. Wiglaf spoke, uttered many fitting words to his comrades; his mind was sad: "I remember that time when we were drinking mead, when in the beer-hall we promised our lord who gave us these rings, that we would requite him for the war-gear, the helms and sharp swords, if need such as this came upon him. He chose us among the host of his own will for this venture, he reminded us of famous deeds and gave me these treasures, the more because he counted us good spear-warriors, bold bearers of helmets, though our lord, the protector of the people, purposed to achieve this mighty task unaided, because among men he had wrought most famous deeds, daring ventures. Now the day has come when our lord needs the strength of valiant warriors. Let us go to help our warlike prince, while the fierce dread flame yet flares. God knows that, as for me, I had much rather the flame should embrace my body with my gold-giver. It does not seem fitting to me, that we should bear shields back to our dwelling, if we cannot first fell the foe, guard the life of the prince of the Weders. I know well that, from his former deeds, he deserves not to suffer affliction alone among the warriors of the Geats, to fall in fight; sword and helmet, corslet and shirt of mail shall be shared by us both."

He went then through the deadly reek, bore his helmet to the aid of the prince, few words he spoke: "Dear Beowulf, achieve all things well, as thou saidst long ago in thy youth, that thou wouldst not let thy repute fail while life lasted; now, resolute chieftain, mighty in deeds,

thou must guard thy life with all thy strength; I will help
thee."

After these words the dragon came raging once more,
the dread evil creature, flashing with surges of flame, to
seek out his foes, the hated men. The shield was burnt
away to the rim by waves of fire. The corslet could not
give help to the young shield-warrior; but the youth
fought mightily beneath his kinsman's buckler, when his
own was consumed by the flames. Then again the war-
like king was mindful of fame; he struck with his battle-
sword with mighty strength, so that, urged by the force
of hate, it stuck in his head. Nægling burst apart; Be-
owulf's sword, ancient and grey, failed in fight. It was not
granted to him that the edges of swords might aid him in
the struggle, when he bore to battle the weapon hard-
ened by blood of wounds; his hand was too strong, he
who, as I have heard, tried every sword beyond its
strength. He was in evil plight.

Then for the third time the enemy of the people, the
bold fire-dragon, was mindful of fighting; he rushed on
the mighty man, when a chance offered, hot and fierce
in fight; he clutched his whole neck with sharp teeth; Be-
owulf grew stained with his life-blood; the gore welled
out in surges.

XXXVII

THEN I HEARD that, in the peril of the people's prince, the exalted earl showed courage, strength and daring, as was his nature. He guarded not his head,[1] but the brave man's hand burned when he helped his kinsman, so that he, the man in his armour, beat down a little the hostile creature; and the sword sank in, gleaming and plated; and the fire after began to abate. Then once more the king himself was master of his thoughts; he brandished the battle-knife, keen and sharp for the fray, which he wore on his corslet; the protector of the Weders cut through the dragon in the midst. They felled the foe; force drove out his life; and then they both had slain him, the noble kinsmen. Such should a man be, a thane in time of need.

That was the last victory for the prince by his own deeds, the end of his work in the world. Then the wound which erstwhile the earth-dragon dealt him began to burn and swell. He found forthwith that the poison was working with pestilent force within his breast. Then the chieftain went till, taking wise thought, he sat down on a seat by the wall; he gazed on the work of giants, saw how the eternal earth-building held within stone arches, firm fixed by pillars. Then with his hands the exceeding good thane bathed him with water, the blood-stained famous prince, his friendly lord, wearied with battle; and loosed his helm.

Beowulf spoke, he talked of his wound, of the hurt sore unto death; he knew well that he had ended his days, his joy on earth. Then all his length of days was passed away, death was exceeding close: "Now I would give armour to my son, if it had been so granted that any heir, sprung from my body, should succeed me. I have ruled this people for fifty years. There was no people's king among the nations about who durst come against me with swords, or oppress me with dread. I have lived the appointed span in my land, guarded well my portion, contrived no crafty attacks, nor sworn many oaths unjustly. Stricken with mortal wounds, I can rejoice in all this; wherefore the Ruler of men has no cause to blame me for the slaughter of kinsmen, when my life passes out from my body. Now, dear Wiglaf, do thou go quickly to behold the hoard under the grey stone, now that the dragon lies low, sleeps sorely wounded, spoiled of the treasure. Haste now that I may see the old riches, the golden treasure, may eagerly gaze on the bright gems of artful work, so that, after winning the great store of jewels, I may the more easily leave life and land, which long I have guarded."

XXXVIII

THEN I HEARD that the son of Weohstan after the speeches quickly obeyed his wounded lord, stricken in battle, bore his ringed corslet, his woven shirt of mail, under the roof of the barrow. Then, exulting in victory, the brave kinsman-thane, as he went by the seat, beheld many costly ornaments, gold gleaming along the ground, wondrous work on the wall, and the lair of the dragon, the old flier at twilight; vessels standing, goblets of olden time, lacking a furbisher, reft of their ornaments. There was many a helm, ancient and rusty, many bracelets cunningly bound. Treasure, gold on the ground, may easily madden any man; conceal it who will!

Likewise he saw a banner all gilt lying high above the hoard, greatest of wonders wrought by hand, cunningly woven in stitches. A gleam shone forth from it so that he might see the floor, behold the jewels. There was no trace of the dragon there, for the sword had carried him off. Then I heard that one man rifled the hoard, the old work of giants in the mound, laid in his bosom flagons and dishes at his own will; took also the banner, brightest of beacons. The sword of the old chieftain—its edge was iron—had earlier laid low him who long while was guardian of the treasures; he bore with him to guard the treasure a dread hot flame, blazing out in battle at midnight, till violently he perished. The messenger was in haste, eager to return, urged on by the treasures. Desire was strong on him to know whether he, the courageous one, should find the mortally-wounded prince of the Weders alive in that place where erstwhile he left him.

Then with the treasures he found the famous prince, his lord bleeding, at the end of his life. Again he began to dash water upon him, until speech came from him. Then the warrior spoke, the aged man in his pain; he gazed on the gold:

"I give thanks in words to the Prince, the King of glory, the eternal Lord, for all the adornments which I behold here, that I have been able to win such for my people before my death-day. Now have I sold my old life for the hoard of treasures; attend ye now to the need of my people. No longer may I tarry here. Bid the men famed in battle raise at the sea-headland a gleaming mound after the burning. It shall tower high on Hroness-ness, a reminder to my people, so that seafarers may afterwards call it Beowulf's barrow when from afar the ships drive over the dark sea."

The prince of brave mind took from his neck a golden ring, gave to the thane, the young spear-warrior, his helm bright with gold, his ring and corslet; bade him use them well: "Thou art the last of our race, of the Wægmundings. Fate has swept all my kinsmen away to their destiny, earls in their might; I must needs follow them."

That was the last word from the old man's thoughts, before he sought the pyre, the hot, fierce surges of flame. His soul passed from his breast to seek the splendour of the saints.

XXXIX

THEN WAS IT sorrow for the young man to see on the earth the man he loved best, his life closed, lying there helpless. The slayer also lay low, the dread earth-dragon, reft of life, vanquished by violence. No longer could the coiled dragon keep guard over the treasure-stores, but iron blades, sharp battle-notched swords, forged by hammers, had carried him off, so that the wide-flier sank to the ground near the treasure-house, still from his wounds. No more did he wheel in his flight through the air at midnight, no more made his appearance exulting in costly possessions; but he fell to the earth because of the warrior's handiwork. Few of a truth among men, among those of might in the land, as I have heard, though they were eager for all exploits, have succeeded in rushing against the blast of the venomous foe, or seizing with hands the hall of rings, if they found the guardian on watch dwelling in the barrow. Beowulf had paid with his death for the many costly treasures; each had gone to the end of fleeting life.

It was not long then till the cowards left the wood, weak failers in loyalty, the ten together, who durst not before wield spears in their lord's great need; but shamefully they bore their shields, the war-gear, where the old man lay; they looked at Wiglaf. He, the foot-warrior, sat wearied, hard by the prince's shoulders, tried to recall him with water. No whit did he succeed; he could not, though dearly he wished, keep life in the prince on earth; nor alter the will of the Almighty. The might of God was pleased to show its power over all men by its deeds, as He yet does now.

Then a grim speech came readily from the youth to those who erstwhile had lost their courage. Wiglaf spoke, son of Weohstan, a man sad at heart; he looked at the hated men: "Lo! he, who wishes to tell the truth, can say that the lord who gave you treasures, warlike adornments, wherein ye stand there, when on the ale-bench he often bestowed on men sitting in hall, a prince to his thanes, helmet and corslet, the most excellent he could anywhere find far or near, that doubtless he miserably cast away the garments of war, when battle beset him. The people's king had indeed no cause to boast of his comrades in fight; yet God, the Disposer of victories, granted that he alone with his sword avenged himself, when he had need of might. Small protection to his life could I afford him in the fight, and yet I tried to aid my kinsman beyond my power. When with the sword I smote the deadly foe, he grew ever weaker, his fire surged out less strongly from his breast. Too few protectors pressed round the prince, when the time came upon him. Now the receiving of jewels, giving of swords, all the splendid heritage, and life's necessities, shall pass away from your race. Every man of the people shall wander, stripped of his rights in the land, when chieftains from afar hear of your flight, the inglorious act. Death is better for all earls than a shameful life."

XL

H<small>E BADE THEN</small> the battle be proclaimed in the entrenchment, up over the sea-cliff, where that troop of earls, bearing their shields, sat sad in mind the whole morning, expecting both issues, the death and the return of the loved man. He who rode on the headland held back little of the late tidings, but truthfully he told them all:

"Now is the giver of delights among the people of the Weders, the lord of the Geats, fast in his deathbed, he bides in his slaughterous couch by the deeds of the dragon. By his side lies the deadly foe stricken with knife wounds; he could not in any way deal a wound to the monster with a sword. Wiglaf, son of Weohstan, sits over Beowulf, the earl over the other lifeless one; reverently he keeps watch over friend and foe.

"Now there is prospect of a time of strife for the people, when the fall of the king becomes widely known to Franks and Frisians. The harsh strife with the Hugas was brought about when Hygelac went to the land of the

Frisians with a navy, where the Hetware laid him low in battle; they did mightily with their greater numbers, so that the corslet-warrior was forced to yield; he fell mid his troops; the prince gave no adornments to his veterans. To us ever since the good will of the Merovingian king has been denied.

"Nor do I expect any peace or good faith from the people of Sweden; for it was widely known that Ongentheow robbed Hæthcyn, son of Hrethel, of life near Ravenswood, when the warlike Scylfings first sought in their pride the people of the Geats. Straightway the aged father of Ohtere,[1] old and terrible, dealt him a blow in return, killed the sea-guide,[2] the old man freed the bride, the wife reft of her gold, the mother of Onela and Ohtere; and then he followed his deadly foes till with difficulty they escaped, leaderless, to Ravenswood. Then he besieged with a mighty host those who had escaped the sword, wearied from wounds; often through the livelong night he threatened the wretched band with misery; he said that in the morning he would do them hurt with the edge of the sword; some on the gallows-tree for the sport of the birds. With dawn came relief again to the woeful, when they heard Hygelac's horn and the blare of the trumpet, when the valiant one came on the track of the warriors of the people.

XLI

"THE BLOOD TRAIL of Swedes and Geats, the deadly attack of men, was widely noted, how the men roused strife between one another. Then the valiant one departed with his kinsmen, the old man very sad, to seek his stronghold. The earl Ongentheow went on further; he had heard of Hygelac's skill in battle, of the proud man's war-strength; he relied not on resistance to check the sea-men, to defend treasure, children and wife against the sea-raiders; the aged man turned thence once more behind a rampart. Then chase was given to the men of the Swedes, the banner to Hygelac. Upon that they overran the stronghold after the people of Hrethel had penetrated the fastnesses. There the grey-haired Ongentheow was constrained to tarry by the edge of the sword, so that the people's king had to suffer the might of Eofor alone. Wulf,[1] son of Wonred, struck him with the sword, so that after the blow the blood gushed from the veins under his hair. Yet was he not daunted, the aged Scylfing, but quickly repaid that deadly stroke with a worse in exchange, as soon as he, the people's king, turned thither. The strong son of Wonred could not give a blow in return to the old man, for he first clove his helmet on his head, so that, stained with blood, he had to give back; he fell on the ground; he was not doomed yet, but he revived, though a wound had stricken him. The bold thane of Hygelac,[2] when his brother was laid low, caused his broad sword, old gigantic brand, to crash the massive helmet over the wall of shields; then the king sank down, the protector of the people; he was stricken unto death. Then were there many who bound up his kinsman; they lifted him speedily when space was cleared for them, so that they might hold possession of the battlefield. Then one warrior spoiled another, took from Ongentheow his iron corslet, his sharp hilted sword, and his helm also; bore the trappings of the old man to Hygelac. He received the adornments, and graciously promised him rewards amid the people, and thus did he fulfil it; the lord of the Geats, the son of Hrethel, when he came to his home, rewarded Eofor and Wulf with exceeding rich treasures for that onslaught; to each of them he gave a hundred thousand measures of land and twisted rings; men on earth had no cause to blame him for the gifts, when they fought heroically; and then to Eofor he gave his only daughter, to adorn his dwelling, as a pledge of good-will.

"That is the feud and the hostility, the deadly hatred of man, which I look for, of Swedish men who will come upon us, when they learn that our prince is dead, who erstwhile guarded treasure and kingdom against foes, the bold Scyldings after the fall of heroes, did what was best for the people, and performed heroic deeds more and more.

"Now haste is best, that we should gaze there upon the people's king, and bring him, who gave us rings, on his way to the pyre. No solitary thing shall be consumed with the brave man, but there is store of treasures, untold gold dearly gained, and now, at the last, rings bought with his own life; the flame shall devour them; the earl shall not wear the treasures as a memorial, nor shall the fair maid bear on her neck the adornment of a circlet, but sad in mind, reft of gold, shall walk in a strange land, not once but oftentimes, now that the leader of the host has done with laughter, joy and merriment. Wherefore many a spear, cold in the morning, shall be grasped with fingers, raised aloft with hands; the sound of the harp shall not rouse the warriors, but the dark raven, ready above the fallen, shall speak many things, shall tell the eagle how he sped at the feasting, when with the wolf he spoiled the slain."

Thus the bold man told evil tidings; he lied not at all in his forecasts and words. The troop all rose up, sadly they went under Earnanæss,[3] with tears welling up, to behold the wonder. Then they found him lifeless on the sand, keeping his helpless couch, him who in former times gave them rings. Then the last of days had come to the valiant one, on which the warlike king, the prince of the Weders, perished a wondrous death. First they saw there a stranger creature, the hateful dragon lying opposite on the ground there; the fire-dragon, the grim dread monster, was scorched with flames; he measured fifty feet long as he lay; often he had taken his pleasure in the air at night; he had come down again to visit his lair; and now he was firm bound by death; he had taken his last delight in the earth-caves. By him stood goblets and flagons, dishes lay there and costly swords eaten through by rust, as if they had remained there a thousand years in the earth's embrace. At that time that mighty heritage, gold of men of olden time, had a curse laid upon it, so that none among men might touch that ring-hall, unless God Himself, the true King of victories—He is the helper of heroes—granted to whom He would to lay open the hoard; even to that man who seemed good unto Him.

XLII

THEN IT WAS clear that the way of them, who had wrongfully hidden the jewels under the wall, had not prospered. First the guardian slew one; then the feud was fiercely revenged. It is unknown where an earl, mighty in valour, may come to the end of life, when he may no longer sit on the mead-bench with his kinsmen. Thus was it with Beowulf, when he sought out the guardian of the barrow and battle; he knew not himself in what way his passing from the world should come about.

Thus did the famous princes, who stored that there,[1] lay a heavy ban upon it till doomsday, so that the man who should plunder the place should be guilty of sins, confined in cursed places, fast in bonds of hell, smitten with plagues. He would rather not have beheld the gold-treasure, the owner's might.

Wiglaf spoke, son of Weohstan: "Often must many an earl suffer sorrow through the will of one, as has come upon us. We could not counsel the dear prince, the protector of the kingdom, not to approach the guardian of the gold, but to let him lie there, where long he had been; bide in his dwelling till the end of the world. We have suffered sore fortune; the hoard is seen, grimly won; that fate was too hard which drew the people's king thither. I was within and beheld all that, the stores of the building, when the chance was granted me; in no pleasant way was a passage opened to me in under the earthwall. In haste I seized a mighty burden of precious treasures in my hands; bore them out hither to my king; he was still living then, wise and clear in mind; the old man in his agony spoke many things, and bade me greet you; ordered that ye should raise on the site of the pyre a high barrow, great and famous, befitting his exploits, even as he was among men the most renowned warrior far and wide throughout the earth, whilst he could enjoy wealth in his castle. Let us now hasten to behold and seek once more the heap of rare gems, the wondrous sight beneath the wall. I will guide you, so that ye may see the rings and broad gold near at hand. Let the bier be made ready, speedily wrought, when we come out and bear then our prince, the loved man, where long he shall wait in the Almighty's keeping."

Then the son of Weohstan, the hero bold in battle, bade orders be given to many of the men who were owners of dwellings, that they, the leaders of bands, should bring from afar wood for the funeral-fire to where the valiant man lay: "Now shall the fire consume—the dark flame shall tower up—the ruler of warriors, him who often endured the iron shower when the storm of arrows, urged with might, darted over the shield-wall, when the shaft did its office; fitted with feathers, it followed the arrow."

In truth the wise son of Weohstan called out the king's thanes from the troop, the best seven together; he went with the seven under the hostile roof of the foemen; one who went in front bore in his hand a torch. It was not settled by lot then who plundered that hoard when the men saw any part unguarded remaining in the hall, lying there perishing; little did any of them mourn that they bore out quickly the precious treasures; also they shoved the dragon, the monster, over the cliff; they let the wave take him, the flood embrace the guardian of the treasures. There was twisted gold beyond measure loaded on the waggon; the chieftain, the grey-haired warrior, was borne to Hronesness.

XLIII

THEN THE PEOPLE of the Geats made ready for him a pyre firm on the ground, hung round with helmets, battle-targes, bright corslets, as he had craved; then the sorrowing men laid in the midst the famous prince, their loved lord. The warriors began to rouse on the barrow the greatest of funeral-fires; the wood-reek mounted up dark above the smoking glow, the crackling flame, mingled with the cry of weeping—the tumult of the winds ceased—until it had consumed the body, hot to the heart. Sad in heart, they lamented the sorrow of their souls, the slaying of their lord; likewise the woman with bound tresses sang a dirge[1] . . . the sky swallowed up the smoke.

Then the people of the Weders wrought a mound, which was lofty and broad, at the edge of the headland, visible far and wide to seafarers; and in ten days they finished the beacon of the man mighty in battle; the remnant of the pyre they compassed round with a wall, as exceeding wise men might most worthily devise it. They

laid on the barrow rings and ornaments, all such adorn-
ments as men, eager for combat, had erstwhile taken
from the hoard; they let the earth keep the treasure of
earls, the gold in the ground, where it yet lies, as useless
to men as it was before. Then men bold in battle, sons of
chieftains, twelve in all, rode about the mound; they
were minded to utter their grief, to lament the king, to
make a chant and to speak of the man; they exalted his
heroic life and praised his valorous deed with all their
strength.

Thus it is fitting that a man should extol his friendly
lord in words, should heartily love him, when he must
needs depart from his body and pass away. Thus did the
men of the Geats, his hearth-companions, bewail the fall
of their lord; they said that among the kings of the world
he was the mildest of men and most kindly, most gentle
to his people and most eager for praise.

NOTES

Chapter I

1. **Scyld-Scefing:** Probably means "son of Sceaf," though the origins of this figure are misty.
2. **misery:** As a child, Scyld arrived in Denmark all by himself, in a ship full of treasure.
3. **whale-road:** The whale-road is the sea.
4. **Beowulf:** Probably refers to the grandfather of the Danish king Hrothgar.
5. **Scyldings:** Descendants of Scyld: the Danes.
6. **rings:** The bestower of rings was the traditional attribute of the generous Anglo-Saxon ruler.

Chapter II

1. **Onela:** Onela was a Swedish king.
2. **lives of men:** Apparently a reference to slaves, whom the king did not have the right to give away.
3. **Heorot:** The word means hart (a deer).

4. **deadly hostility:** The great hall would later burn to the ground in the midst of struggle between Ingeld and his father-in-law, Hrothgar.
5. **mighty spirit:** The monster Grendel.
6. **minstrel:** The Anglo-Saxon word is *scop,* the classic bard of epic poetry.

Chapter III

1. **hall-visitant:** Grendel.
2. **bought off:** In ancient Germanic law, a killer could only obtain peace from the family whose offspring he had murdered by the payment of compensation money, or *wergild.*
3. **purpose:** As an outlaw, Grendel could not address the King of the Realm.
4. **slayer of souls:** The Devil. The basic narrative framework of the poem is Christian, despite the omnipresence of pagan reference and the pagan world.

Chapter IV

1. **Hygelac's thane:** Beowulf, nephew of Hygelac, the great Geat lord.
2. **swan-road:** The sea. Another example of a kenning, the Anglo-Saxon verbal device of juxtaposing two or more nouns to form a fresh metaphoric combination, e.g., *whale-road, world-candle.*

Chapter V

1. **boar-images:** Carved images of boars, sometimes clothed like humans, were added to helmets in the belief they would increase the power of the wearer.

Chapter VI

1. **haughty hero:** Wulfgar, herald and officer of King Hrothgar of the Danes.

Chapter VII

1. **Hrethel of the Geats:** Father of Hygelac and grandfather of Beowulf.
2. **prince of the Bright-Danes:** Beowulf adopts the traditionally humble posture toward his liege, from whom the hero will expect compensation.
3. **protect my head:** Bury my body.
4. **Weland:** The blacksmith of the Norse gods.

Chapter VIII

1. **he:** Ecgtheow; Hrothgar had settled this man's feud with the Wulfings.

Chapter XII

1. **high hall:** The chief purpose of such a hall as Heorot was wining and dining in the heroic male manner.

Chapter XIV

1. **mere:** Lake.
2. **son of Wæls:** Father of Sigemund.
3. **Heremod:** An initially brilliant king of the Danes who became greedy and cruel and eventually had to take refuge with the Jutes, who killed him. He was

thus overshadowed by Sigemund and became the prototype of the cruel and ineffective ruler.

Chapter XV

1. **son of Ecglaf:** Unferth, who taunted Beowulf but then eventually loaned him his precious sword, Hrunting.

Chapter XVI

1. **treachery:** In the later history of the Danes, after the death of Hrothgar, his nephew Hrothulf drove Hrothgar's son and successor from the throne.
2. **friends of Ing:** Ing was a legendary Danish king, and his friends were the Danes.

Chapter XVII

1. **sons of Finn:** The scop's tale, which follows, is allusive and hard to follow. Some light is shed on it by another Old English poem, *The Fight at Finnsburg*.
2. **Hildeburh:** Hildeburh was the sister of the ruling Danish king, Hnæf. She was married to the king of the Jutes. Hnæf and a party of Danes made what was presumably a friendly visit to Hildeburh and her husband at their house in Finnsburg. A deadly quarrel broke out between the Jutes and the Danes, and in the course of it Hnæf and the son of Hildeburh and Finn were killed.
3. **conditions:** It is not entirely clear who is offering the conditions, but it seems likely that the Jutes are doing

so, given their weakened state after the battle at Finnsburg. The peace imposed on the Danes the painful agreement to live in harmony with the Jutes, who had just killed the Danish king, Hnæf.

4. **Folcwalda:** Finn.
5. **warlike Scyldings:** Hnæf.
6. **mounted up:** The body of Hildeburh's son was placed on the funeral pyre.

Chapter XVIII

1. **stronghold:** This seems to refer to the surviving Jutes.
2. **Hunlafing:** The son of Hunlauf, a Dane who had been killed in the battle with the Jutes, makes a symbolic gesture by laying the sword of his father in the lap of Hengest, the Danish leader who had directed the battle against the Jutes. Hengest would later assault the Jutes again and kill their leader, Finn.
3. **kindly words:** The manuscript is corrupt and impossible to interpret at this point.

Chapter XIX

1. **Brosings:** The fire dwarves of Scandinavian mythology. They made a splendid necklace worn by the goddess Freya; it was later stolen by the Dane Hama.
2. **the ring:** Later accounts say that Beowulf gave the ring to Hygelac's queen, Hygd, although here it is said that Hygelac was wearing the ring during the ill-fated expedition against the Jutes.

Chapter XXII

1. **son of princes:** Hrothgar.
2. **the son of Ecglaf . . . spoke:** Another reference to Unferth.

Chapter XXIV

1. **gaped wide:** Grendel is decapitated.

Chapter XXV

1. **Heremod:** Earlier Danish ruler whose cruelty to his people was legendary, and whose ultimate fate—to be killed by the Jutes with whom he sought exile—was exemplary.

Chapter XXVIII

1. **he:** Beowulf.
2. **Hygd:** Bride and queen to Hygelac.
3. **Thryth:** The reference that follows may be to the queen of the fourth-century king Offa. Thryth, who was so cruel she had her suitors put to death if they so much as looked into her face, is presented as a total contrast to Hygd.
4. **who was meant to establish peace:** Women were frequently married to the rulers of unfriendly countries in order to weave a peace with them. In this sense Thryth was a "weaver of peace."
5. **a good famous woman:** A fourth-century Angle king, ancestor of the famous English king Offa of Mercia.

6. **mighty in onslaught:** By praising the offspring of the early king Offa, the poet indirectly praises King Offa (died 796).

Chapter XXIX

1. **Ongentheow:** Swedish king, ultimately defeated by Hygelac (uncle of Beowulf) and killed by Eofor.
2. **Froda:** King of the Heathobards (a Germanic tribe living on the South Baltic coast), father of Ingeld.
3. **feuds and struggles:** The feuds between the Danes and the Heathobards.

Chapter XXX

1. **gleams the armour:** That is, the Heathobards have the bitter pleasure of seeing, on their Danish guests, the brilliant armor that the Danes had taken from them in battle.
2. **bride's thane:** That is, Freawaru's attendant, who is wearing the armor of the father of his Heathobard attacker.
3. **pouch:** A sack to put his victims in.

Chapter XXXI

1. **Heorogar:** Older brother of Hrothgar, by whom he was succeeded as king.
2. **despised:** The only reference in the poem to the earlier life of Beowulf, who as a youth was despised by his people.
3. **sword of Hrethel:** Hrethel was a Geatish king, father of Hygelac.

4. **Heardred:** Son of Hygelac; Heardred succeeded his father as king and was later killed by the Swedes.
5. **enraged:** The text is badly corrupted at this point and impossible to interpret.

Chapter XXXII

1. **seized him. . . . :** Several words are missing from the text at this point.

Chapter XXXIII

1. **Hetware:** Frankish tribe that fought with the Jutes to defeat Hygelac and the Geats.
2. **rule the realm:** Beowulf refused to accept royal power as direct successor to Heardred.
3. **Weder-Geats:** Beowulf remained a faithful supporter of Heardred.
4. **Ohtere:** Swedish king, son of Ongentheow. At Ohtere's death his throne was taken over by his brother Onela, who drove out Ohtere's sons. Ultimately Onela, defeated at the Geatish court by Heardred, surrendered the throne to Beowulf.

Chapter XXXIV

1. **wretched Eadgils:** Eadgils was a Swedish prince, son of Ohtere. Beowulf helped Eadgils win the Swedish throne from his uncle Onela, a usurper whom Beowulf eventually killed.
2. **raven:** The raven, along with the wolf and the eagle, was the traditional creature to eat the corpses and remains of the dead in battle.

Chapter XXXV

1. **Hæthcyn:** Hæthcyn was the son of Hrethel, king of the Geats. Hæthcyn was succeeded by Hygelac after being killed in an attack on the Swedes.
2. **he:** Hygelac.
3. **Gepidæ:** A Germanic tribe known as a source of mercenaries.

Chapter XXXVI

1. **Ælfhere:** Of the same Geatish family as Beowulf, Wiglaf will be the true support of Beowulf in the slaying of the dragon.
2. **he:** Weohstan.

Chapter XXXVII

1. **his head:** The dragon's head.

Chapter XL

1. **Ohtere:** Ongentheow.
2. **sea-guide:** The Geatish king, Hæthcyn.

Chapter XLI

1. **Wulf:** A Geat wounded by Ongentheow at Ravenswood.
2. **thane of Hygelac:** The Geat Eofor.
3. **Earnanæss:** The headland near where Beowulf fights the dragon.

Chapter XLII

1. **that there:** The treasure.

Chapter XLIII

1. **dirge:** Words are missing from the text.

INTERPRETIVE NOTES

The Plot

Beowulf opens with the tale of Scyld, a mythical Danish king. After the recital of his deeds, his people fit out a funeral ship with "great costly stores," and lay the mysterious king's body within. Then, they "let the ocean bear him; they surrendered him to the sea." The image of this magical sea burial will return at the end of the epic, with Beowulf's own noble funeral. The heart of the poem concerns the mysterious and heroic deeds that join the two funerals.

In broad terms, this is the story: The Danish king Hrothgar has a large feasting hall (Heorot) set up in the royal compound, a center of light and civilization. For twelve years, a terrible monster named Grendel has been ravaging the hall and the court's inhabitants; in fact, when we join the story, thirty men have just been devoured in one of the monster's night raids.

We are introduced to Beowulf while he is still at home

in the kingdom of the Geats, a Germanic tribe dwelling in southern Sweden, and near neighbors to the Danes and the Swedes. When he hears of Grendel, Beowulf resolves to go to Hrothgar's aid. When he and his men arrive at the Danish kingdom and explain their intended mission they are welcomed and feasted by Hrothgar.

After many crises and heroic deeds, the victorious Beowulf returns with his men to Heorot. Hrothgar once again praises them with formal speeches, showers them with splendid guest gifts, and tearfully accedes to their request to return home. Beowulf and his fourteen faithful comrades sail home, tell tales, accept honors, and settle down in Geatland, basking in the admiration of Beowulf's ruling uncle Hygelac.

In part two of our tale, Beowulf has been ruling over the Geats for fifty years as king of the Geats. Once again a monster—a fire-breathing dragon—is threatening civilized life. The dragon's treasure hoard has been robbed by a runaway slave, and the creature is infuriated. Beowulf is called back into action and a series of bloody crises, near escapes, and heroic acts ensue. Beowulf finds himself pushed to the limit in combat with the dragon, even with the aid of his faithful ally Wiglaf, who sticks by him to the end. At the close of our tale, Beowulf is buried with a state funeral, his funeral mound inside filled with lethal riches of the dragon's hoard.

Characters

Beowulf. Son of Ecgtheow, who is the daughter of Hrethel and sister of Hygelac. Beowulf is a fearless cleanser of evil, and one who offers himself when there is a threat afoot. He is modest and loyal, true at all times to his chief patron, Uncle Hygelac in Geatland. His hearth companions praise him as "among the kings of the world . . . the mildest of men and most kindly, most gentle to his people and most eager for praise."

Hygelac. Beowulf's uncle, husband of Hygd. He dies defeated by the Franks, wearing the necklace gotten from Hrothgar. A man of honor and dignity.

Hrothgar. A major king of the Danes. He builds Heorot and rewards Beowulf for his courage in conquering Grendel. He is the brother of Heorogar. Though given to expatiating, this elder is wise and measured in his judgements.

Wealtheow. Danish queen, wife of Hrothgar; she asks Beowulf to help her sons if Hrothgar dies.

Wiglaf. A Wægmunding (member of prominent Geatish family), like Beowulf. This true and reliable friend helps Beowulf slay the dragon.

Onela. Swedish king, brother-in-law of Hrothgar; later conquered and slain by Beowulf.

Hygd. Queen of the Geats and wife of Hygelac. She receives the necklace Hrothgar gives to Beowulf. After Hygelac's death, she offers the kingdom to Beowulf. A gentle and noble lady.

Unferth. A Dane, son of Ecglaf and retainer of Hrothgar. At first he taunts Beowulf but later lends him his sword, Hruntung. Mercurial, but capable of learning and growing.

Heorogar. Hrothgar's elder brother, whom Hrothgar follows as king of the Danes. It is his armor which is given to Beowulf by Hrothgar.

Heremond. An early ruler of the South Danes, and a classic evil king.

Hengest. A Half-Dane who follows Hnæf, and whom he avenges by killing Finn.

Grendel. A cannibal monster who attacks Heorot and Hrothgar's Danish kingdom for twelve years. A figure of pure evil, attracted to the reveling hall, but only in the hope of filling his stomach.

Symbols and Themes

Light versus Darkness. The tale of *Beowulf* emerges from a northern land where the sun virtually disappears for months on end. A deep concern with light and warmth still permeates northern cultures today: imagine the impact of the Heorot feasting hall in midwinter, raising its flames to combat twenty-three hours a day in darkness. It is no wonder, then, that the sun—or *world-candle,* as it is called in Anglo-Saxon—is seen as the center of God's creation, and a benevolent eye that looks down on the known world. Almost all sources of light are positive stalwarts against the ever impending dark and cold. As the poem puts it, "the Almighty wrought the world, the earth bright in its beauty which the water encompasses; the Victorious One established the brightness of sun and moon for a light to dwellers in the land. . . ." The great man-made fires of the feasting halls and the funeral pyres are symbols of valiant civilization, joy, and defiance.

Outside the world of light there is a world not only of complete but of terrible darkness. That is the world in which Grendel—"the mighty spirit who dwelt in darkness"—and his mother lurk. It is also the world into which Beowulf descends when he goes down into the cave of Grendel's mother to fight with her to the death. (The land surrounding the evil mere is "an eerie place . . . thence the surge of waves mounts up dark to the clouds, when the wind stirs up hostile storms til the air darkens, the skies weep.") Beowulf rises into the light, upward through the dark mere, after killing Grendel's mother and chopping Grendel in half. The darkness from which Beowulf rises is emblematic of the evil and ogreish world which lies on all sides, threatening civilized society.

Civilization versus Barbarism. Beowulf is the emblem of the civilized man, both in his brash youth and fifty years later as king of the Geats. The strength of his hands equals that of thirty men, and he is a tireless defender of the good. But out in the dark, Beowulf has much to combat, and he undertakes what he does, not as an Eagle Scout but as a practical realist skilled in purging foul evil. It's a good thing he is realistic: the darkness is filled with opponents of civilization—the descendants of Cain, "all evil spawn, ogres and elves and sea-monsters, giants too, who struggled a long time against God." It is against all these evils that Beowulf is pitted. It is no wonder that Beowulf was taken to be an allegorical figure by some of the early Christian critics of the poem. He is not only on the side of light but on that of the Lord, who had slain Cain for the murder of Abel and thereby released the hatred of the descendants of Cain. Beowulf, like the narrator, is privy to the secrets of "the Lord, the Judge of deeds." The benighted Danish knights in Heorot, however, "wist not the Lord God; nor in truth could they praise the Protector of the Heavens, the Ruler of glory."

Age versus Youth. The abrupt aging of Beowulf in the second half of the poem has troubled scholars, some of whom think the epic of *Beowulf* is composed of several separate poems joined together. Whether or not this is the case, it is clear that the *Beowulf* poet, or whoever put the present epic together, made a stark decision. He juxtaposed brash, heroic youth—as a very young man Beowulf was despised by his community as a person of small importance—with the sagacious wisdom of the beloved, gentle Beowulf of the end of the poem. The same polarity appears throughout the epic. For example, the wisdom of Hrothgar and Hygelac, the two elders of the Danes and Geats, is contrasted with the obstreperous behavior of Unferth, who impudently challenges Beowulf upon the warrior's arrival among the Danes. The association of wisdom with age is deeply rooted in Beowulf's patriarchal society, where age and experience are essential to gaining life-mastering skills. This association makes all the more beautiful the preternatural wisdom of Beowulf when first we see him as a young conquering hero in the foreign land of the Danes.

Water and Land. The North European–Germanic culture from which *Beowulf* emerges is surrounded by ocean at every turn, and its kingdoms are basically seafaring communities. There is a constant polarity in *Be-*

owulf between the realms of water and land. This division gives a unity both of theme and imagination to the epic, which is constantly moving from one place to another across the North Sea and around mysterious misty coasts, and semidefined landmasses. We can see this in the parallelism between the beginning and the end of the epic.

At the outset of *Beowulf,* Scyld-Scefing, the king of the Danes, has died and is being released to the sea in his funeral ship in a touching and powerful scene that embodies the giving and receiving grandeur of the ocean. Scyld's comrades "bear him out to the shore of the sea." They lay down the loved lord "by the mast," surrounded by his treasures, "that were to pass far with him into the power of the flood." This mysterious passing away mirrors the equally mysterious arrival of Scyld among the Danes when he was a child. "No whit less did they furnish him with gifts, with great costly stones, than did those who sent him forth in the beginning while he was still a child alone over the waves." What the sea gives, mysteriously, returns to the sea.

At the conclusion of *Beowulf,* a funeral mound is prepared "lofty and broad, at the edge of the headland, visible far and wide to seafarers." Beowulf's body, there in the sight of seafarers who pass, is consumed by the flames, along with all of his most precious material possessions. Like Scyld, Beowulf vanishes from the earth, a heroic memory consuming its materiality along with itself.

CRITICAL EXCERPTS

Historical/Political/Linguistic Contexts

Chambers, R. W., *Beowulf: An Introduction to the Study of the Poem with a Discussion of the Stories of Offa and Finn* (Cambridge: The University Press, 1921).

An exhaustive (628 pages) life-work study of the cultural and historical setting of *Beowulf* in the larger picture of Scandinavian literatures and early English history. Still exemplary as a reference work.

The unique MS [manuscript] of *Beowulf* may be, and if possible should be, seen by the student in the British Museum. It is a good specimen of the elegant script of Anglo-Saxon times: "a book got up with some care," as if intended for the library of a nobleman or of a monastery. Yet this MS is removed from the date when the poem was composed and from the events which it narrates (so far as these events are historic at all) by periods of time approximately equal to those which separate us from the time when Shakespeare's *Henry V* was written, and when the battle of Agincourt was fought . . . To try to penetrate the darkness of the five centuries which lie behind this extant MS by fitting together such fragments of illustrative information as can be obtained, and by using the imagination to bridge the gaps, has been the business of three generations of scholars distributed among the ten nations of Germanic speech. A whole library has been written around our poem, and the result is that this book cannot be as simple as either writer or reader might have wished.

Klaeber, Fr., *Beowulf and The Fight at Finnsburg* (Boston: D.C. Heath and Company, 1922).

A wonderfully clear and detailed study of the text of *Beowulf*, its language and linguistic features, and its folklore and historical contexts. Includes a complete Anglo-Saxon text of the poem, with glossary.

The work left behind by the anonymous author does not rank with the few great masterpieces of epic poetry. *Beowulf* is not an English *Iliad*, not a standard Germanic or national Anglo-Saxon epos. In respect to plot it is immeasurably inferior to the grand, heroic Niebelungenlied. Yet it deservedly holds the first place in our study of Old English literature. . . . As an eloquent exponent of old Germanic life it stands wholly in a class by itself. As an exemplar of Anglo-Saxon poetic endeavor it reveals an ambitious purpose and a degree of success in its accomplishment which are worthy of unstinted praise. In noble and powerful language, and with a technical skill unequalled in the history of our ancient poetry, it portrays stirring heroic exploits and, through these, brings before us the manly ideals which appealed to the enlightened nobles of the age. It combines the best elements of the old culture with the aspirations of the new.

Wardale, E. E., *Chapters on Old English Literature* (London: Routledge and Kegan Paul, 1935).

A highly literate survey, concentrating on poetry (as distinct from prose, most of which in early English is derivative from foreign sources).

The subject matter of *Beowulf* contains both historical and fabulous elements. It has grown up out of a union of history and folk-tale. As had already been said, most of the persons and many of the events dealt with have an historical basis. They are mentioned by independent Latin writers or in O.N. [Old Norse] documents which may be considered reliable for the main facts, or in later Latin writings based on such documents. The figure, however, of the hero Beowulf himself cannot be traced, and his feats against Grendel, the hag, and the dragon, as well as some other incidents, are obviously taken from folk-tale.

Anderson, George K., *The Literature of the Anglo-Saxons* (New York: Russell and Russell, 1962).

A classic literary history employing the tools of political and cultural history, archaeology, and linguistics to set a context for the development of early English literature.

Even if one discounts the usual amount of conventional boasting in which Beowulf, as any good epic hero, indulges before a combat, there still remains an aura of confidence about him which is extraordinary. Neither the grim ferocity of the "mighty merewife," Grendel's mother, nor the flames pouring from the head of the fire-dragon dissuade Beowulf from his advance into danger. If there is any appreciable flaw in his character—any tragic defect of body or spirit which brings about his downfall, such as Achilles or Siegfried or Roland suffered—it is a superabundance of this valor and a resulting overconfidence which prompts him to sally forth against the fire-drake with inadequate protection at a too advanced age.

Literary Interpretations: 1930s–1960s

Tolkien, J. R. R., "Beowulf: The Monsters and the Critics" (1936), reprinted in Fry, Donald, *The Beowulf Poet* (Englewood Cliffs, NJ: Prentice-Hall, 1968).

This often reprinted essay by Professor Tolkien is a brilliant defense of *Beowulf* against those critics who think it a great but badly constructed poem.

In *Beowulf* we have, then, an historical poem about the pagan past, or an attempt at one—literal historical fidelity founded on modern research was, of course, not attempted. It is a poem by a learned man writing of old times, who looking back on the heroism and sorrow feels in them something permanent and something symbolical. So far from being a confused semi-pagan—historically unlikely for a man of this sort in the period—he brought probably *first* to his task a knowledge of Christian poetry, especially that of the Caedmon school, and especially *Genesis*. He makes his minstrel sing in Heorot of the Creation of the earth and the lights of Heaven. So excellent is this choice as the theme of the harp that maddened Grendel lurking joyless in the dark without that it matters little whether this is anachronistic or not. Secondly, to his task the poet brought a considerable learning in native lays and traditions: only by learning and training could such things be acquired; they were no more born naturally into an Englishman of the seventh or eighth centuries, by simple virtue of being an "Anglo-Saxon," than ready-made knowledge of poetry and history is inherited at birth by modern children.

Creed, Robert, "The Making of an Anglo-Saxon Poem" (1959), in Martin Stevens and Jerome Mandel, *Old English Literature: Twenty-Two Analytical Essays* (Lincoln, NE: University of Nebraska Press, 1968).

A much-cited essay on the oral formulaic pattern of choices which go into the making of a poem like *Beowulf*.

I cannot attempt to deal in so brief a study with the way in which the singer puts together the larger elements of his poem. I shall therefore take only a very small portion of Beowulf, eight verses (four lines), and attempt, by means of references to similar verses and lines in the rest of the poem and in other surviving Anglo-Saxon poems, to illustrate the thesis that the making of any Anglo-Saxon poem was a process of choosing rapidly and largely on the basis of alliterative needs not between individual words but between *formulas*.

Whitelock, Dorothy, "The Audience of Beowulf" (1964), in Martin Stevens and Jerome Mandel, *Old English Lit-*

erature: Twenty-Two Analytical Essays (Lincoln, NE: University of Nebraska Press, l968).

This article treats the cultural context of *Beowulf* in its own time.

> And why my title? It will seem very trite and obvious to say that the effect of any work of art depends not only on the author's power and skill, but also on what is already present in the minds of its hearers, or readers, or—in the case of the visual arts—its beholders. Nevertheless, this consideration is particularly pertinent in the poem of *Beowulf,* partly because it is far removed from us in time, so that we are not entitled to assume without investigation that an audience of the poet's day would be moved by the same things as we are, or, if by the same things, in the same way; but still more, because much of the poem is composed with a subtle technique of allusion, reminder, and suggestion, so that we cannot guess at the effect the poet was hoping to attain unless we know something of the meaning and associations his hints and allusions carried for those for whom he composed his poem.

Irving, Edward B. Jr., *A Reading of Beowulf* (New Haven: Yale University Press, l968).

A fascinating study of the theme of the negative in the heroic epic of *Beowulf.* From stress on the element of loss, of not-having or not-being, the book moves to acute understanding of the real value of the hero in *Beowulf.*

> Openness is one part of the courtesy—more than courtesy, tact—which is evident in these early speeches of Beowulf. His appeal to the coastguard for

advice, his admission that the rumors the Geats have heard about Grendel might very well not be true, his presenting himself at this point merely as a well-meaning advisor to Hrothgar who might be able to suggest a plan whereby Hrothgar could overcome Grendel—all illustrate this quality of tact. For, as a foreign champion whose very presence is potentially an insult to a humiliated people, Beowulf must not only disarm the Danes' hostility but he must gain acceptance from them, and gain it from each individual he encounters.

Crossley-Holland, Kevin, and Bruce Mitchell, *Beowulf,* translated and introduced (New York: Farrar, Straus and Giroux, 1968).

In their introduction, Crossley-Holland and Mitchell discuss the importance of reading *Beowulf* as a poem, rather than a piece of prose.

> *Beowulf* is a poem. One of the most pleasing trends in recent Old English studies has been an increasing awareness of the truth and importance of this simple observation. But it is one which has often been overlooked by scholars and critics, some of whom have professed to regard *Beowulf* as a museum for the antiquarian, a sourcebook for the historian, a treatise for the student of Christian thought, or a gymnasium for the philologist. Those who have treated it as one of these things have helped the Grendel of criticism to devour the poem in the presence of generations of students.

Brodeur, Arthur Gilchrist, *The Art of Beowulf* (Berkeley: University of California Press, 1969).

A fine study of the artistry and unified imagination of the epic of *Beowulf*.

The three great events of the main plot—the killing of Grendel, the victory over Grendel's dam, and the fight with the dragon—display striking structural similarities, and equally striking variety of narrative treatment. In each case, the inciting cause is very much the same: the destruction wrought by a monster; in each, the hero, after a hard and dangerous struggle, slays his foe—though the hero himself is fatally hurt in his last fight. In each, the fight is preceded by an exposition of the hero's state of mind; the fights with Grendel and his dam are each followed by his report of the combat to Hrothgar, and by an account of the gratitude and praise heaped upon him by the Danish king. Each of Beowulf's monster-killings is undertaken to deliver a people sorely afflicted; and in each case the people involved, though saved from present affliction, is nevertheless doomed to suffer ultimate catastrophe.

Irving, Edward B., Jr., *Introduction to Beowulf* (Englewood Cliffs, NJ: Prentice-Hall, 1969).
An excellent introduction to the background and literary development of the text of *Beowulf*.

A hero is a man, and somehow more than a man. Wiglaf and the grieving Geats see Beowulf as a man known and loved well by them; the Messenger sees him as a tangible felt presence in the solid world of history; when Beowulf reminisces about his life, we feel we know him better than we have known him be-

fore in the poem. The poet never lets go of this real
and personal dimension to the very end. Yet a myste-
rious and half-mythic atmosphere surrounds the fu-
neral rites, perhaps largely because we half-recognize
the striking of those same notes of feeling we heard
in the description of Scyld's funeral at the beginning
of the poem.

Literary Interpretations: 1970s–1990s

Berger, Harry and H. Marshall Leicester, "Social Struc-
ture as Doom: The Limits of Heroism in *Beowulf*"
(1974), in Robert Burlin and Edward Irving, *Old English
Studies in Honour of John C. Pope* (Toronto: University
of Toronto Press, 1974).

A subtle and extensive essay on the rich form the
heroic ideal assumes in *Beowulf*.

[Beowulf] is, by the end of the poem, domesticated
into a beloved culture hero. Taming that wilderness,
like conquering Grendel, is exchanging bad dreams
for good. Of what use is it to bring forth such dreams
from the earth, or from the folk imagination with its
powerful longing for mystery, terror, beauty, and
peace? Beowulf appeases the folk longing; his strange
but consoling image answers the dread and passivity,
dispels the ennui, that gave rise to it. A dream of Be-
owulf might relax and enervate the poet's audience
just as Beowulf unstrung the Geats and Hrothgar the
Danes. Between the *scop* [storyteller] and his subject
matter, between the audience and the poem, reci-
procity has to be possible. The *scop* reciprocates by
revising, and we reciprocate by remaining alert, re-

fusing to be lulled by the heroic dream, listening attentively for the sounds of doom working within the social order.

Donahue, Charles, "Potlatch and Charity: Notes on the Heroic in *Beowulf*," in *Anglo-Saxon Poetry: Essays in Appreciation* (Notre Dame: University of Notre Dame Press, 1975).

An outstanding study of the spirituality of *Beowulf*, which expresses itself in part through an obsession with the ancient practice of gift-giving.

Perhaps the *Beowulf* poet's greatest imaginative achievement was to body forth such an image of an heroic and good but non-Christian Germania as enabled him—and doubtless some of his audience—to reconcile admiration for ancient heroic ancestors with a new Christian faith. The poet, influenced by pre-Augustinian theological views of human history, portrayed his non-Christian Germania as an essentially good society, whose members followed the natural law engraved in their hearts and looked with gratitude towards God, Whose existence they had discovered by considering His works. There were heathens in this society. Heathens are men who seek the aid of evil spirits and who do not know the true God. Such was Grendel, and doubtless Grendel's dam. Such were also the Danes who sacrificed at heathen shrines. The heathens, however, are the antagonists in the poem. They are opposed to God and given over to evil practices, such as murder and refusal to pay wergild. The protagonists, however, true representatives of Germania in days of yore, Hrothgar and most of the

Danes, Beowulf, Hygelac, and, so far as knowledge goes, all of the Geats, were those who knew God and followed the law of nature. . . . There are no good pagans in the poem.

Gardner, John, *The Construction of Christian Poetry in Old English* (Carbondale, IL: Southern Illinois University Press, l975).

A brilliant study of the Christian motifs in Old English poetry, and their direct influence on the literary structure of *Beowulf*. Here the author makes a subtle point about the difference between the God of *Beowulf*'s world, and Christ, who has conquered death.

The trouble with vengeance as compensation for the loss of felicity is tragically shown in Hrethel's house. One of Hrethel's sons kills the other by accident, and in such a case no avenging of the slain man is thinkable. Even the wisdom of Hrothgar would fail here. God's favor may send some comfort to a king in need of a champion, but no champion known to pagans can raise the dead or turn back the sorrow borne in mutability itself. This is the significance of Beowulf's successive confrontations with monsters. God in his wisdom can enable a shrewd and valiant hero to overcome the enemy of rational order, Grendel. And the God who won the war with the giants can enable a man to overcome perverse Power, the perverted irascibility of Grendel's dam, whose loyalty is not to Law but to an outlaw. But the prerevelation God of Hrothgar and Hygelac cannot overcome mutability itself, the destructive principle inherent in matter, slave to Fate—the principle traditionally represented in the figure of the dragon.

Frank, Roberta, "The *Beowulf* Poet's Sense of History," in *The Wisdom of Poetry: Essays in Early English Literature in Honor of Morton W. Bloomfield*, ed. Larry Benson and Siegfried Wenzel (Kalamazoo, MI: Mediæval Institute Publications, 1982).

A canny and subtle essay on the *Beowulf*-poet's insistence on the layered time-setting that separates him in his present from the events he describes in his epic.

> Awareness of historical change, of the pastness of a past that itself has depth, is not instinctive to man; there is nothing natural about a sense of history. Anthropologists report that the lack of historical perspective is a feature of primitive thought, and historians that its absence characterizes mediaeval thinking . . . Morton Bloomfield has shown that a sense of history, even a tentative, undeveloped one, was a rare thing in fourteenth-century England, and that Chaucer's attention to chronology and his preoccupation with cultural diversity have affinities with aspects of the early Italian Renaissance. But what in the Anglo-Saxon period stimulated a monastic author to stress the differences between ancient days and his own, to paint the past as if it were something other than the present? The *Beowulf*-poet's reconstruction of a northern heroic age is chronologically sophisticated, rich in local color and fitting speeches.

Lapidge, Michael, "Beowulf and the Psychology of Terror," in *Heroic Poetry in the Anglo-Saxon Period: Studies in Honor of Jess B. Bessinger, Jr.*, ed. Helen Damico and John Leyerle (Kalamazoo, MI: Mediæval Institute Publications, 1993).

An illuminating study of the horrible—especially of the horror of the undead, or zombie—in *Beowulf*.

The Beowulf-poet clearly realized that instinctual human fear results from the perception of monstrous creatures that lie outside familiar conceptual categories (and hence are unknowable, or "uncanny" in Freud's term). That is why he carefully avoided supplying any kind of precise visual description of his monster, so that what eventually approached Heorot would be sensed as something truly horrific because totally unfamiliar. The horror resulting from the threatening approach of unfamiliar monsters is experienced most intensely in nightmares, and it is no coincidence that the poet described his monster in terms evocative of the *nihtgengan* of nightmares.

Frantzen, Allen, *Before the Closet: Same-Sex Love from Beowulf to Angels in America* (Chicago: University of Chicago Press, 1998).

An absorbing study of the role of the homoerotic in corners of Western literature and art traditionally thought untouched by such predilections.

I wish to examine briefly the elements of the "language of erotic poetry" . . . and to see what Anglo-Saxon literature in *Beowulf* and elsewhere tells us about affection or displays of emotion between men, especially between fathers and sons. The key elements in the passage include tears, the kiss, the embrace that follows, and especially the old king's "secret longing for the dear man" . . . What is the nature of this longing, and why does Hrothgar keep his longing secret? Does he in fact do so? A secret longing—a longing for Beowulf that "burns" in Hrothgar's blood but that the king cannot acknowledge—might well be sexual.

Heaney, Seamus, *Beowulf: A New Translation* (New York: Farrar, Straus and Giroux, 2000).

A new translation, by a Nobel Prize–winning Irish poet, with Old English and translation on opposite pages and a revealing introduction.

I came to the task of translating *Beowulf* with a prejudice in favour of forthright delivery. I remembered the voice of the poem as being attractively direct, even though the diction was ornate and the narrative method at times oblique. What I had always loved was a kind of foursquareness about the utterance, a feeling of living inside a constantly indicative mood, in the presence of an understanding that assumes you share an awareness of the perilous nature of life and are yet capable of seeing it steadily, and, when necessary, sternly.

QUESTIONS FOR DISCUSSION

Beowulf is the story of a hero. Are hero stories still popular today? Can you think of some examples of heroes in fiction or film who set out to overwhelm evil—and succeed? Are these people truly knights in shining armor, without ulterior motives? What about real-life heroes—what motivates them? Desire for some kind of reward, pure love of mankind, hatred of evil?

Can you think of any popular books or movies today that seem like they have been influenced by the world portrayed in *Beowulf*? What seem to be the primary values of that world?

What kind of evil do Grendel and his mother represent? Why does Beowulf consider it so important to destroy these foes? How does Beowulf's sense of evil differ from yours, or from that of our world? How do we define evil?

How do the competing world views of Christianity and

paganism show up in *Beowulf*? Do the characters seem to be more Christian, or more pagan? How can you tell?

Is the dominant tone in the entire epic of *Beowulf* pessimistic? At the end of the poem do you feel that the future will be better than the present, or worse? What, if anything, has changed?

How do the "action" scenes in *Beowulf* compare to those in the movies of today? Are they longer or shorter, bloodier or more restrained? What can we tell about the tastes of early audiences of *Beowulf* based on the style of these battle scenes?

Suggestions for the
Interested Reader

If you enjoyed *Beowulf*, you might also be interested in the following:

Grendel, by John Gardner. A 1971 novel written from the viewpoint of Grendel by a former professor of medieval culture and literature. It gives us insight into both the text of *Beowulf* and into the world as seen through the eyes of a monster.

The Lord of the Rings, by J. R. R. Tolkien. Now also a trio of acclaimed films, Tolkien's famous trilogy about Middle Earth draws on some of the Nordic legends that also undergird Beowulf's world. Tolkien was also a medievalist.

Eaters of the Dead, by Michael Crichton. Crichton is the author of several works of popular fiction, including *Jurassic Park*. *Eaters of the Dead* was inspired by *Beowulf* and loosely based on the fragments of a journal of an Arab man who traveled north with a band of Vikings in the tenth century to fight a myterious evil in their homeland. It is an exciting novel, set roughly at the same time as *Beowulf*, full of fascinating period detail. A film version, titled *The 13th Warrior*, appeared in 1999.

The Mists of Avalon, by Marion Zimmer Bradley. This bestselling 1982 novel retells the well-known story of King Arthur (a figure, like Beowulf, who wrestled with both pagan and Christian influences) from the point of view of his half sister, the witch Morgaine. It is a purely fictional retelling, of course, influenced very little by actual archaeological research on King Arthur, but it is an interesting reversal of the usual morality surrounding the life of the legendary king.

BESTSELLING ENRICHED CLASSICS

JANE EYRE
Charlotte Brontë
978-0-671-01479-7
$5.99

WUTHERING HEIGHTS
Emily Brontë
978-0-7434-8764-1
$4.95

THE GOOD EARTH
Pearl S. Buck
978-0-671-51012-1
$6.99

**THE AWAKENING AND
SELECTED STORIES**
Kate Chopin
978-0-7434-8767-2
$4.95

**HEART OF DARKNESS
AND THE SECRET SHARER**
Joseph Conrad
978-0-7434-8765-8
$4.95

GREAT EXPECTATIONS
Charles Dickens
978-0-7434-8761-0
$4.95

A TALE OF TWO CITIES
Charles Dickens
978-0-7434-8760-3
$4.95

**THE COUNT OF
MONTE CRISTO**
Alexandre Dumas
978-0-7434-8755-9
$6.50